DAREDEVIL

Thank you!

Linda S. Browning

Other Books by the Author

LESLIE & BELINDA MYSTERIES
Shanghaied
Rambler
Coming August 2017
The World's Longest Yard Sale - is Murder

Pickett House: Tennesee Haunting Fiction

PARLOR GAME MYSTERIES
Coming April 2017
Hanging Tobacco

DAREDEVIL

A LESLIE & BELINDA MYSTERY

by

Linda S. Browning

Includes Bonus Short Story

NO WAKE

Buddhapuss Ink • Edison NJ

The short story "No Wake" was previously published in the book *Mystery Times Ten 2013* published by Buddhapuss Ink LLC in 2013.
Cover Art © Svetlanaprikhnenko | Dreamstime.com
Cover and Book Layout/Design by The Book Team
Editor, MaryChris Bradley
Copyeditor, Andrea H. Curley
ISBN 978-1-941523-12-4 (Paperback Original)
First Paperback Edition May 2017

The Buddhapuss Ink LLC name and logos are trademarks of Buddhapuss Ink LLC. www.buddhapussink.com

Learn more or contact the author at:

Facebook: LindaSBrowningAuthor
Twitter: @LindaSBrowning
Website: lindabrowning.net

DEDICATION

My LESLIE & BELINDA MYSTERIES will forever be dedicated to my best friend since the summer before we entered the eighth grade. Lynne, these are for you.

I want to thank all the oddball people who have inhabited my life thus far: family, friends, neighbors, enemies, et al. Some are no longer with us, but their eccentricities live on.

No Wake

wake *noun* \ˈwāk \ : the track left by a moving body (as a ship) in a fluid (as water); *broadly* : a track or path left

~ *Merriam-Webster*

Lake water is nasty. I'm a look-at-the-lake person and not a play-in-or-on-the-lake person. I live in a townhome on Lake Manchester in Tennessee. The lake is beautiful. I like to look at it. I have no desire to touch it. When I was a kid, I loved being in the water. It didn't matter whether it was a lake or a pool. Now there is no way that I would swim in a lake…my lake…any lake. I mean, fish and frogs poop, don't they? They have to go somewhere…and guess where?

My husband, Tom, and I retired to Fairlawn Glen eight years ago. When we started looking for a place to retire, I told Tom that Fairlawn sounded like the name of a cemetery. As it turns out, Fairlawn Glen is a great place for retirees, even though it is practically a residency requirement to keep a walker on your premises at all times.

Three years after we moved from Michigan, Tom dropped dead on the golf course on the thirteenth hole. Massive heart attack. Dead before he hit the ground. Dead man falling. I am sixty-eight years old now. Tom was eight years older than I. Still, it was a shock. Oh, I'm Leslie Barrett, by the way. It was not a shock, however, that Tom had died while on the golf course. Tom was always on the golf course. I hated playing golf. I really tried to like it, but my Lord, golf is boring.

It hadn't helped that Tom always insisted on starting out early in the morning. I don't like mornings. Tom knew that. Morning progresses like a disease. The acute stage is around 6:00 A.M. (agony is excruciating)…the chronic stage is around 8:00 A.M. (pain is only dulled by massive amounts of caffeine)…around 10:00 A.M., morning goes into remission. I quit playing golf when Tom forbade me to drive the golf cart. There are warning signs on the road to alert the old people of "golf cart crossings," and the posted speed limit around here is only thirty miles an hour. This one time I decided that I could beat the approaching car, so I gunned it…as much as you can gun a golf cart. I beat that car by a mile. Tom wouldn't let me drive the golf cart after that. He said I was reckless. Tom tried to get me interested in fishing for a while. It was kind of fun…until I saw a snake. That-Was-So-Over. Do snakes poop? Probably. The snake was in the lake, of course.

I get bored easily. Since Tom was always out golfing, I was at loose ends. I know perfectly well that there are a lot of places around here where old people can volunteer their services, and the causes are worthy. The problem is that I do not now—nor will I ever—consider myself to be an "old people"…and when I work, I want to be paid.

Next, I tried the "Wellness Center." That's what they call the exercise club around here. I tried to like that too. They have every kind of exercise machine you can think of in there. The problem is, people keep touching them.

I "worked out" on a treadmill for a couple of months. I figured that I could push the buttons with a towel and never make skin contact. That lasted until some man next to me started humming. Really loud. HMMMMM. HMMMMM. For God's sake, just shut up and walk. I abandoned the machines and moved on to the swimming pool, which glistened, pristine with chlorine. AHHHHH. I would swim for my exercise. After happily swimming for about three months, I was stopped short in the lobby in complete shock. Big as life stood a sign:

THE POOL IS TEMPORARILY CLOSED
DUE TO FECAL CONTAMINATION.

What? Shit. Somebody pooped in the pool? That was it for me. Honey, there isn't enough bleach or chlorine in the world that could get me back in that water.

Thank God I met Belinda. I'm five feet two inches and weigh around 130 pounds. Belinda is close to six feet tall and weighs…more than I do. She is a couple of years older than I am, and she is my best friend in the entire world. Belinda may not be my physical twin, but psychically we are identical.

Belinda's husband, Frank, died two years ago. It was a sad time. To be perfectly honest, I didn't much like Frank. He was a big blowhard, a real know-it-all. Obviously the know-it-all didn't know what copious amounts of Scotch could do to a guy's liver. Scare up some onions 'cause that sucker was good and fried. Frank died. It was sad.

Belinda and I like to keep up on the local news. Concerned and involved citizens, you could call us. Or nosy and pushy mature (not old) broads, if you prefer. We look into curious situations and then make a big deal out of nothing. That is how it started last month with the lake dredging. Belinda and I attend all the scheduled townhome community meetings. It was at the meeting in March where it was announced that our lake was scheduled for dredging in June. Dredging? For what? This sounded exciting. So we gathered information from knowledgeable sources. We called Mrs. Towers. Mrs. Towers is an eighty-five-year-old widowed lady (must be an epidemic) who lives in one of our townhome units. If it needs to be known, she knows it. We wonder about her sources; nevertheless, if you wanted the skinny, you asked Mrs. Towers. Evidently, the lakes are dredged every ten years as a matter of routine maintenance. Maintenance? Of what? Water? How do you maintain water? It isn't like you have to mow it or anything.

It turns out that sediments and gunk build up in man-made lakes (I may not have mentioned it before, but Lake Manchester is a man-made lake…that doesn't make the water any less nasty), and there are machines that scoop out the gunk that collects at the bottom of the lake; then the gunk gets hauled off, and the lake is happy again. Still, the entire process was supposed to take an entire month, and there would be these huge machines and a bunch of guys. It was like waiting for Christmas.

• • •

Last summer we spent one entire afternoon watching a bunch of construction workers dig this enormous hole a couple of streets over. I had this theory that it was a mass grave (my imagination tends to run to the dark side). I envisioned a white van (serial killers' vans are always white) pulling up to the freshly dug hole in the dead of night and the killer unloading his macabre cargo. Covering the bodies with a layer of dirt so the construction men wouldn't notice them, and the next morning all traces would be concreted over. It was brilliant. The victims were likely hookers. Serial killers always kill hookers (and then carry them off in white vans).

It turns out that they were digging a basement; it was fun while it lasted. It was fascinating to watch though. And the fellas were nice.…

• • •

Finally it was June, and we were into the second week of dredging. Every afternoon Belinda came over to my unit, and she and I, and Riff-Raff, would watch the dredging guys. They were set up at the marina across the lake because the beach allowed them access for the scooper machine. Riff is my four-year-old Maltese mixed with some other kind of small dog. Riff doesn't weigh but ten pounds, but don't tell her that. She's the size of a purse, but she thinks she's a killer.

My patio faces the lake across a large lawn. There are several docks lined up, and every one of them has a pontoon boat. Our lake is what they call a "no wake" lake. No jet skis, no motorboats with people water skiing…no sir. No fun allowed on our lake. Pontoon boats. Big whoop. They are like big, bloated bars of soap floating around with deck chairs. You hardly ever see one out on the lake unless it is over a summer holiday and the kids and grandkids are in for a visit. Waste of money as far as I am concerned. Belinda, Riff, and I were sitting on my patio drinking lemonade. Well, Belinda and I were drinking lemonade. Riff had a bowl of water. Very clean water. So, we were sitting and watching the dredging guys. It really is interesting. They have this huge machine with a big scooper on a crane—like a steam shovel—and the entire machine floats. Don't ask me how. It must weigh a ton. Anyway, it putters around (leaving no wake, of course) scooping up stuff from the bottom of the lake and then putters over to dump the stuff in this huge bin. After every dumping, two men poke around in the gunk with some poking equipment to make sure they haven't scooped up any innocent bystanders. One time, after much poking, the two men hauled out this humongous snapping turtle by its tail.

This afternoon we were watching the dredging guys, and suddenly there was this big commotion around the dumping bin. Belinda and I perked right up. We thought maybe it was another turtle…but guys started running around like crazy. The man operating the scooper machine clambered down to look in the bin. He started yelling and waving his arms. Belinda and I could see him. Well, I could. I had the binoculars.

Belinda and I passed the binoculars back and forth throughout the remainder of that afternoon. We saw several police cars and then, finally, a coroner's van. Oh my.

Before the police cars and the coroner van arrived, a bunch of the dredging guys started throwing up. I had to give the binoculars to Belinda. I can't do disgusting. Belinda can do disgusting. She was a nurse. I was a social worker. Give me a good, clean emotional crisis any day.

• • •

I found a dead body once. I was working in home health and went to see Mrs. Weatherford. I knocked and rang the doorbell and then *whoo-hooed* upon entering. I *whoo-hooed* my way through the house into the bedroom. There she was. Mrs. Weatherford was on the bed facing me. Eyes wide-open, with blood trickling out one corner of her mouth.

I got out of there. I called the office on my cell phone—which back in those days was the size of a small suitcase. I spoke with one of the nurses. She asked me, "Are you sure she's dead?"

"Yes, she's dead."

"Did you take her pulse?"

"God, no."

"Then how do you know she is dead?"

"Look," I said, "she's either dead, or she has the best poker face that I've ever seen."

Mrs. Weatherford was, indeed, dead. I was convinced that it had been murder because of the blood trickle. The nurses explained to me that the blood trickle was consistent with Mrs. Weatherford's medical condition and cause of death and all, so once I was convinced that it hadn't been murder, I lost interest. Oh, don't get me wrong—Mrs. Weatherford was dead and all, and it was sad.

• • •

When Belinda told me that a coroner's van had pulled up, I wrestled the binoculars away from her. This could get emotional. Two guys got out of the back of the van with a stretcher and one of those black body bags like you see on TV. Body bags are always black, and serial killers' vans are always white. It is important to be observant.

After the police cars and the coroner's van pulled away, the dredging guys went back to work. Belinda and I were jumping out of our skins. Riff was on point...barking in the direction of the marina. She could smell it. It was murder.

We called Mrs. Towers. She didn't even know about it. Belinda and I high-fived. We had finally scooped Mrs. Towers. We settled back and allowed our source to ferret out the details. We watched our community newspapers, but they never publish any real news. Everybody was sick of reading about the overpopulation of Canadian geese—as though we couldn't see them. Mrs. Towers promised to keep us in the loop.

• • •

One week after the big discovery, Belinda and I had just gotten our observation station in place when Mrs. Towers called.

The body had been identified as Abner Cummings. "Abner?" I said. "How do they know?"

"What?" Belinda interrupted.

I shooed her away with my hand. "Uh-huh…uh-huh."

"What?"

I shooed again.

After hanging up, I relayed the news.

"The body has been identified as Abner Cummings."

I had barely begun to tell her when Belinda sucked in her breath and turned pale.

"Belinda…what's wrong. Are you okay?"

"A-b-ner? How do they know it is Abner?"

"The medical examiner traced the ID number on his hip implant."

Abner Cummings lived in the townhome next door to Belinda. He was a nice old man. An eighty-nine-year-old widower. Abner was as sharp as a tack. He had very strong views and wasn't shy about sharing them. Abner also fell down a lot. His head was covered with so many stitches and staples that he could have gone to a Halloween party as Frankenstein's monster without need of a costume.

"Belinda, you are as white as a ghost; have some lemonade."

Belinda took several ladylike sips. When she had composed herself, she asked, "How did he die?"

"Well, I'd guess lying around on the bottom of the lake could have had something to do with it."

"Leslie," Belinda said in a strangled voice. "This isn't funny. Abner's dead."

"I didn't realize you were...um...close to Abner."

"He was my neighbor."

"He was my neighbor too. But I swear you look like you might faint." Abner Cummings had lived in Fairlawn Glen for thirty-five years. Abner moved into our townhome complex after his wife's death ten years ago. Belinda and Frank moved in seven years ago. As I mentioned before, Frank died two years ago. Do the math.

"Abner was lonely," Belinda said softly.

I finally got it. "Belinda...you mean that you and Abner...""

"No, no, Leslie. Don't be ridiculous. The man was eighty-nine years old and I'm seventy, for heaven's sake."

"So? Were you and Abner, um, friends while Frank was alive?"

"Of course."

"I can't believe that you've been carrying on with Abner Cummings all this time and didn't tell me!"

"I have not been 'carrying on' with anybody. And if I were...of course I would tell you."

I was only somewhat mollified.

"Sometimes we would sit on his patio and drink iced tea or something. He would get my mail if I was out of town and vice versa. I assumed he was still in Florida."

We had all made the same assumption.

Every November Abner flew down to Florida and spent the winter with his daughter. The last time I could remember seeing Abner Cummings was at the community meeting last September. It had been a fiery one because someone was there from the Tennessee Department of Transportation (TDOT) to inform residents about the long-antic-ipated widening of two-lane Trendle Road to four lanes. Most people living out here are all in favor of widening the road. It is the only thoroughfare that connects Fairlawn Glen with the big city. The old people out here drive like…old people, and it is impossible to pass any of them. Every vehicle appears to be piloted by one of the Muppets.

Abner was strongly opposed to the four-lane, as it would require the destruction of the Baptist church that Abner had attended for the last thirty-five years. The church would be paid handsomely for the ac-quisition and another church would be built at a location close by, but Abner was morally outraged that his church would have to come down in order to accommodate the road. He was always distributing petitions. I heard that Abner had collected enough signatures on his petition (most were church members) to get some kind of injunction that at least would postpone the start of the venture.

"Remember how angry Abner got at the September meeting with the road people?" I asked.

"Yes…Abner is, *was*, very passionate about his church." Then Belinda surprised me by chuckling. "Remember what he said to that new guy who moved in last summer with that great big motor on his pontoon boat?"

"Oh my goodness, yes. That was so funny!"

Abner had started a ruckus with new-guy because the outboard motor on his boat was so big…horsepower and all. Abner lectured him about how "no wake" is allowed on Manchester, implying that new-guy was going to go roaring up and down the lake with his big motor. When new-guy denied that he had any intention of roaring, Abner had demanded loudly, "Well, what's the purpose of having a big motor if you don't intend to use it?"

New-guy responded, "I can have as big a motor as I want to; I just can't go very fast!"

Belinda and I got the giggles with that exchange and had to leave the room. We laughed again now at the memory.

We watched the dredging guys for a few minutes until I said, "Okay, we have to assume that poor old Abner was murdered."

Belinda immediately started shaking her head. "Oh no you don't. You are not going to start running around promoting murder theories."

Which, of course, was exactly what I was intending to do. Belinda, bless her heart, always tried to balance my imagination with logic, but logic, schmogic. Abner Cummings had been murdered. How else could he have gotten stuck at the bottom of the lake? It didn't make sense. It wasn't like he was found floating around as if he had fallen off a boat or something. Where was the boat? Where were the witnesses? No doubt about it; it was murder.

• • •

"It had to be his daughter," I announced two days after the gruesome discovery.

"Why do you say that? Life insurance or something?" asked Belinda.

"Exactly. We all thought Abner was safely ensconced in his daughter's home in Florida, and now we find out he has been 'sleeping with the fishes' all this time. Why didn't she report him missing? Something about this whole thing smells…and it isn't just Abner."

Belinda moaned, and Riff whimpered.

"We have to look at motive," I said. "The most likely motive for murder is money."

"How do you know?" Belinda huffed.

"I pay attention, Belinda. I read," I huffed back at her.

Belinda started tapping her finger on the side of her glass of lemonade.

"What is it?" I asked. I know this woman so well.

"Nothing."

"Don't give me that, Belinda. You've thought of something."

"Well, Abner's daughter is the only surviving relative that I am aware of, so she will have to come up here to clear out his home. Maybe we could watch for her and ask her some discreet questions."

"You mean like, why in the hell didn't you report your father missing?"

"Well, yes. Why don't we call Mrs. Towers and see if she knows anything."

I gave her a smug smile. "I already did. The daughter is supposed to be here tomorrow."

We decided that Belinda would keep an eye out for the daughter the next day and call me as soon as she spotted her.

• • •

I was on pins and needles all that night and the next morning. Belinda finally called me at 2:00 P.M. Shoot. Because I'd been hanging around the telephone waiting for her call, I'd missed an entire day of dredging.

I hurried right over to Belinda's, and we went next door. Knocking briefly, we whoo-hoo-ed our way inside. The daughter, April, was in her late fifties or early sixties, and she was really nice. I had been all set to accuse her of murder, so I wasn't prepared to like her.

Belinda and I offered our condolences.

April sniffed back tears. "Dad was close to ninety, but to lose him like this…"

I very gently interrogated her…I was a social worker…I know how to be gentle. "We all thought Abner was in Florida with you. Didn't you wonder when he didn't show up?"

April told us that she and Abner corresponded by e-mail. Her father didn't like to talk on the telephone, so once he had mastered the art of e-mail, they spoke (so to speak) often. He e-mailed her last November to tell her that he had decided to stay in Tennessee over the winter, as he didn't think he was up to the trip. Abner reminded her that he *was* getting on in years.

"When do the authorities think he died?" I asked gently.

"The medical examiner is guessing that Dad died five to six months ago. Cause of death was difficult to determine due to the circumstances—you know. The autopsy did show that he had a skull fracture. So they are thinking he must have been out on the dock and slipped and hit his head or something. After that, the hypothesis is that snapping turtles—you know, they can get really big out here."

Belinda and I concurred. I saw one crossing the road heading toward our lake one summer that was as big as a footstool.

She continued. "They think the turtles, um, grabbed hold of him; and once he got pulled under, he got hung up on one of those stumps that are submerged in the lake. Then the dredging equipment dislodged…" The poor thing broke down in tears.

It's true that the bottom of the lake is littered with tree stumps. People who fish around here are always complaining about their lures getting hung up on them. And no, I have no idea how tree stumps get on the bottom of a lake…but obviously they do.
"Yes, dear." I patted her shoulder gently. "We know."

When April had recovered somewhat, Belinda asked, "Weren't you curious when you never heard from him again?"

"That's what's really odd. Dad and I e-mailed back and forth all winter. His e-mails didn't stop until a couple of weeks ago, and then… well…you know what happened then."

"Do you still have the e-mails, dear?" I asked.

She shook her head. "No, unfortunately. I delete e-mails almost immediately. But they should still be on Dad's computer."

Oh boy. We were closing in now.

"Where is his computer?" I asked.

"Leslie…" Belinda warned, but I ignored her.

We followed April into a back room where Abner had kept his computer. "I don't know whether it is password protected, but I doubt it," said April.

"May I?" I asked…gently.

"Of course," she responded.

I settled myself at the keyboard and booted up the computer (that's computer jargon for I turned it on). The e-mail account was active, but there had been zero activity since last November. The last e-mail on record—and yes, I checked the trash place—was the e-mail Abner had reportedly sent to his daughter announcing his intention to stay in Tennessee over the winter.

April couldn't explain it. "Someone must have erased them. But why?"

"What about his regular mail?" Belinda asked.

"I went to the post office. They said Dad stopped his mail delivery in November…just like every winter." Belinda and I believed April was telling the truth. Something was verrrryyy wrong. A bit of further snooping revealed that Abner's utility bills were set up for automatic payment with his bank. A very tidy murder.

We left April to her lonely task.

Now that Belinda was on board the mystery train, we headed back to her place to make some discreet inquiries. Belinda called our source and brought her up to date on the case. Mrs. Towers was impressed with what we had uncovered. She told us that the police were still investigating Abner's death but were leaning toward ruling it accidental. She suggested we tell the police about the missing e-mails.

I called, and a police officer said they already knew there was no record of e-mails on Abner's computer. He was actually quite insulting about it…implying that we were pretty stupid to suggest that they hadn't thought to look.

That made me mad, so I said to the officer, "Well, if you are really smart, you will have a forensic expert examine the hard drive!" I know that computer data is never totally erased from a hard drive. I watch a lot of *NCIS* with that cute Mark Harmon. I really impressed Belinda with my knowledge of computer stuff. The officer pooh-poohed my suspicions by suggesting that the daughter was mistaken somehow, or embarrassed that she hadn't kept in contact with her father.

When I hung up, Belinda asked, "What are they going to do?"

"Nothing," I harrumphed. "They're going to write off poor old Abner as accidental turtle fodder."

"Oh my Lord!"

"Belinda, it looks like it is up to us to find out who murdered your boyfriend."

"Abner was not my boyfriend!" When Belinda gets excited, she sometimes shrieks like Edith Bunker. "Oh, never mind."

Belinda and I got down to the onerous job (well, not really onerous…I enjoy a good project) of listing potential suspects who had motivation to kill Abner. It wasn't a very long list.

We ruled out angry husbands because it was unlikely that Abner was dallying his dilly in anyone else's dally. According to Belinda, Abner's dilly couldn't dally even if he had wanted it to. Of course, Belinda claims this was only supposition. I decided not to pry… A lady is entitled to *some* secrets.

We ruled out April. She was too nice to have been involved with murder. Belinda and I both pride ourselves on the accuracy of our bullshit meters, and we detected none.

We considered the new guy and his *big* outboard motor. Abner was well known as the no-wake Nazi, and he had gotten pretty hot under the collar at the meeting in September. It didn't sound like much of a motive though. We decided to make a list of all the townhome residents. We immediately ruled out Belinda and me, Mrs. Towers, and…well, Abner, of course. Abner had had some heated exchanges with other residents during meetings…especially about the planned four-lane.

"Belinda, you said you have a key to Abner's place because you used to get his mail?"

"Yes."

"I have an idea. We didn't search his computer very well for clues. All we did was establish that Abner's e-mails to April stopped in November. We didn't look at e-mail history."

"I don't know, Les. It's a good idea though. Why don't you call that police officer and suggest they do an e-mail search."

I snorted in a very unladylike fashion and waved my arm dismissively. "Barney Fife could crack this case before any of those clowns even get close."

"Peek out and see if April is still over there," I instructed.

Belinda peeked. "Her van is gone."

"Get the key, Belinda. Let's go. If we don't move fast, she will disconnect the computer."

We hustled next door and into poor old Abner's den. I booted up (that means, oh, never mind, I already told you) the computer and clicked on the little man silhouette with ABNER next to it. Belinda pulled up a chair, and we started peeling back the layers of e-mails. We got bored. A bunch of e-mails back and forth with April (as she had indicated) and lame jokes from friends. He had e-mailed a lot with fellow church members. We opened those (for forensic purposes) and read them, but they were mostly comments about the sermons and choices of hymns. Those Baptists take their hymn choices very seriously. I'm Catholic. In and out in half an hour. Belinda is Methodist. I went with her once to one of her services. I'd rather play golf.

One e-mail in particular caught my eye. It was a heated exchange back and forth about the anticipated four-lane and the petitions that Abner was forever circulating. The e-mail came from some guy named

Mitchell Gaines. This Mr. Gaines was obviously all in favor of the four-lane. He stressed the convenience for residents (finally, a chance to pass one of the Muppets), but he also mentioned (several times) the financial benefits to commercial enterprises along the road. This Mr. Gaines even pointed out that the Baptist church was more than forty years old, and the congregation would only benefit from the construction of a new church.

Belinda had been correct when she said that Abner was passionate about his church. His return e-mails railed against the capitalistic motivations of TDOT and the business owners along the route, who selfishly stood to make money from the sale of their properties.

"I wonder who this Mr. Gaines guy is. He sounds plenty upset," said Belinda.

"I've got an idea," I said excitedly.

"What are you going to do?" Belinda asked suspiciously. Poor Belinda, she is always so tentative.

I opened a new e-mail. "We are going to throw out a teaser to Mr. Gaines and see what we get."

I typed, "We know who you are and what you did to poor old Abner." I hit SEND.

"Oh my God, Leslie. Are you out of your mind? Delete it…delete it before it gets sent."

"Give it a few minutes, Belinda. If this guy answers, it will be a good indication that he is involved somehow."

We sat there for a good twenty minutes. Nothing. We got bored. I'm no computer genius, but as far as I could tell, the message had been received.

"Let's go, Leslie. This is making me very nervous."

The computer dinged. We had mail!

I opened the e-mail, which said, "Who are you? Abner's dead."

"Oh my God, Leslie! Let's go. Let's go."

"No. Let's wait around for a few minutes. See if he sends another e-mail. Don't you think *you* at least owe it to Abner to find out what happened to him? Let's wait and see what else this guy has to say."

Fortunately, I had brought Riff with me (I always bring Riff with me—almost everywhere—that's the advantage of having a purse-size dog), so I didn't have to worry about getting right home.

Belinda's voice was nearing the Bunker shriek. "*I* don't owe Abner anything! I told you; we were just friends."

"Still, if I were murdered, I would hope you would at least try to find out who done it."

Belinda knew when she was beaten. With a huge sigh she capitulated. "One hour. We leave after one hour."

"Agreed."

We waited around for an hour. We were getting really bored. Riff was having a great time with all the fascinating new smells. I let her wander around. Who knew; maybe she would turn up some evidence with her doggy sniffer.

"He's not going to say any more, Les. Let's go."

"Give it a few more minutes…" I started, and then stopped with a sharp intake of breath.

There was someone at the front door.

"Oh my God," Belinda whisper-shrieked (if you think that is easy… try it).

"Riff…" I whisper-called to my dog. "Come here, Riff." Riff trotted right back to me, and I scooped her up.

Belinda and I crept out of the den. "It's probably just April coming back," I whispered reasonably. "Don't panic."

We were halfway across the living room heading toward the patio when the front door opened. We had neglected to lock it.

A great big fat man stood in the doorway leaning heavily on a walker.

Okay, I thought. This doesn't look too bad. Belinda, Riff, and I can easily take this guy.

The fat man stumped his way into the foyer. A younger man followed. Uh-oh.

"Dad, get out of the way," the younger man said in an exasperated tone. When he had shoved his way around the fat man, he leveled a severe gaze our way. "What's going on here?"

I was starting to get mad. I straightened up and leveled right back at him. "We know what you did to poor old Abner. The police will be here any second." Then I narrowed my eyes at the fat man and declared smugly, *Mr. Mitchell Gaines!*

The fat man started to blubber, "It was an-n-n ac-ci-dent."

"Shut up, Dad."

"No… I can't s-stand this any longer."

"What happened?" Belinda whisper-shrieked.

"Shut up, Dad."

The fat man stumped his way past his son and leaned heavily on the walker. "I own the strip mall off Trendle," he explained. "Abner wouldn't leave things alone. He just kept up with his stupid petitions and letters to TDOT. I've been losing money on that strip mall for years. Half of the stores are empty. I *need* the money from the sale of that land. We only came over that night to talk with Abner…to reason with him."

"Shut up, Dad," the younger man growled.

Riff growled back at him. I was so proud.

The fat man kept talking. "We got into an argument. I got so worked up that Brian was afraid I was going to have a heart attack. Brian gave him a little push."

"Dad…" Brian and Riff growled in unison.

"Abner just kind of crumpled. He hit his head on the corner of the end table. We could tell he was dead."

Belinda had been inching toward the patio door with two fingers pinching my shirt, pulling me along.

"We panicked," blubbered the fat man. "Brian took Abner down to the docks and threw him in the water. We figured he would be found in the morning."

The rest of it fell into place. I said solemnly, "When the body wasn't found, Brian hacked into Abner's computer and set up the e-mail trail with his daughter in order to stall for time. Then when Abner got dredged up, Brian erased the e-mails."

The fat man nodded. He gave a blubbering growl. "Damn turtles."

I frowned at Brian. "But you couldn't have known that April automatically purged her e-mails?"

"No." Brian gave me a creepy smile. "That was most cooperative of her."

Belinda wrenched open the door to the patio and practically threw me through the screen door. Brian immediately started break dancing his way around his fat father. Belinda slammed the patio door behind her and pushed the barbecue grill up tight against the screen door to slow him down.

"Run, Leslie!" Belinda shrieked. My best friend took off across the lawn, headed for the docks. She was running like a track star. I was close (well, not real close) behind her. I heard little whimpering noises as I ran. I shut up when I realized it was me.

We ran past Mrs. Towers, who was sitting in the middle of the lawn watching the dredging guys.

I heard the grill screech across the patio. I managed to bawl as I passed Mrs. Towers, "They're after us."

Belinda was hotfooting it down (what we called) the boardwalk. She was untying new-guy's boat from the mooring when I panted up beside her clutching Riff. I glanced behind us crazily. Mrs. Towers had wheezed her way up out of her chair and was trying to engage Brian in some sort of stalling maneuver by planting herself and her walker in front of him. The fat man was batting at the barbecue grill with his walker.

Belinda shrieked, "Get in the boat, Les!"

"But...but..." I sputtered.

"GET. IN. THE. BOAT," Belinda shrieked even louder.

So I GOT. IN. THE. BOAT. I gave Riff a soft toss, and then I jumped (well, I didn't actually jump. If it had been caught on a YouTube video, I imagine I would have looked quite comical.) in the boat behind Belinda and Riff.

By this time Brian had run around Mrs. Towers and made his way to the boardwalk.

"We don't have a key," I wailed. Belinda was already at the wheel. I heard the engine start up. I hurried to her side. "Where did you get the key?"

Belinda was already moving away from the dock. Over her shoulder she explained, "Frank and I used to have a boat. Everybody hides a key under the dash."

By the time Brian got to the dock, we were too far away for him to do anything about it. He quickly jumped (now, *he* did jump...the murderous young show-off) onto another boat.

He never had a chance though. Belinda had chosen new-guy's boat with its big outboard motor. Sometimes bigger is better.

"Hold on to something!" Belinda shrieked. When we got farther from the dock, she floored it. Riff and I were crouched down beside her. I had one arm around Riff and the other wrapped around the pilot's chair.

VA-ROOM!!! It was glorious. Riff and I hung on for all we were worth. I rose up enough to peer behind us. Brian was following in his pathetic little no wake boat. He never had a chance. I turned around and peered fearfully over the dash.

"You're going to hit the scooper guy!" I shouted. We watched the scooper guy jump out of his scooper machine and into the nasty, dredged-up lake water. I cringed.

Belinda maneuvered around the scooper machine like a pro. She zigged and zagged. She was fabulous. We were headed for the beach. Quite a crowd of dredging guys had gathered on the beach to watch the action.

"Stop…Belinda…stop!" I yelled. "We're going to crash."

"I can't stop!" Belinda shrieked.

"What do you mean, you can't stop!?"

"Frank only let me drive. He never let me dock."

Riff and I sank to the floor of the boat again. "Oh…great…" I moaned aloud. Belinda's dead, blowhard husband was going to get us all killed. I never did like Frank.

Belinda turned off the engine. "Get up, Leslie. We have to jump."

"Jump?! Are you crazy?!" The boat was already slowing down but was still wobbling toward the beach.

"You do what you want to, but I'm jumping!" Belinda clambered up on the side of the boat, and over she went.

"Oh God…oh God…oh God," I whimpered as I grappled my way up and over the railing. I clasped Riff so tightly in one arm that she yelped. I screwed up my eyes, pinched my nose tightly, and made a leap of faith after my friend.

I lost my hold on Riff when we hit the water. I came up flailing and gasping. Riff paddled up to me and, once she was sure I was okay, headed for the beach. I dog paddled right behind her.

Belinda had reached the beach and was being helped out of the water by a couple of the dredging guys. Riff reached the beach and was furiously shaking water from her fur. By now I was on my hands and knees, gasping. I was suddenly swooped from the shallow water. One of the dredging guys had me in his arms. Oh my. Sometimes there are advantages to being a small woman. Nobody had swooped up Belinda.

I was so weak that I had to wrap my arms around the dredging guy's neck and lay my head against his dredging-guy chest. Oh my.

Belinda had already directed the dredging guys to call the cops. We made our way into the coffee shop of the marina, where we awaited the police, wrapped up in big towels and sipping hot coffee. New-guy's boat was floating aimlessly just off the beach. Brian had long since given up the chase. My dredging guy was holding Riff. Nothing is sexier than a big dredging guy cuddling a ten-pound purse dog.

Brian and his fat father were arrested. Belinda and I were famous. Mrs. Towers was so proud. We don't know what charges will be brought against the men. I suspect the actual death really had been an accident. Abner should have worn a helmet just to go out to the mailbox. Dumping him in the nasty lake water like so much turtle kibble, however…well, that's just wrong.

• • •

A few days after our adventure, Belinda, Riff, and I were back on my patio, sipping lemonade and watching the dredging guys. Riff and I had taken so many baths, we squeaked when we breathed. Like I said, lake water is nasty. I had the binoculars trained on the scooper machine and watched as it puttered back to the gunk bin.

I muttered, "I wonder how many more people have gone missing around here?"

"Leslie…" Belinda cautioned.

When I lowered the binoculars and narrowed my eyes at her, I saw that she was grinning.

"Let's call Mrs. Towers," suggested my best friend.

DAREDEVIL

Chapter One

dare·dev·il *adjective* \ˈder-ˌde-vəl\: recklessly and often ostentatiously daring.

daredevil *noun*: a person who does dangerous things especially in order to get attention.

~Merriam-Webster

There should be a federal law requiring real estate agents to warn people about bears. When my husband, Tom, and I were researching areas of the country with climates more temperate than our native Michigan, I'm fairly certain that man-eating carnivores appeared in the *Do Not Want* column of defined criteria. We ruled out Florida because of the alligators. Those cold-blooded creatures were turning up in swimming pools and trailer parks! We also ruled out all states with tarantulas; those states alleged to have *dry* heat. I prefer not to live in an oven…with or without spiders.

Our agent was very upfront about the forest-dwelling critters in Middle Tennessee—for the most part, they came with the temperate climate.

I was confused by her reference to *Middle* Tennessee. "Why is the area referred to as *Middle* Tennessee?"

She gave me a look that could only be described as abject pity for such a dense Yankee woman. "Because the Cumberland Plateau is in the middle of the state of Tennessee, honey."

When I opened my mouth to seek further clarification, Tom suggested that I defer to the colloquial definition of the territory. "Leslie, they have championship golf courses, no alligators, no tarantulas, and no known cases of spontaneous combustion. Did I mention that they have championship golf courses?"

When I did my own research, I learned that the state has three divisions: Western Tennessee, Middle Tennessee, and Eastern Tennessee. I liked the sheer simplicity with which the state divides itself. Western, Eastern, and everything in the middle is the Middle. You gotta love it.

So, we came to settle in Lake Manchester Town-homes in Middle Tennessee—nestled amid a woodsy area inhabited by Disney-esque furry things such as squirrels, chipmunks, bunny rabbits, and deer. She warned us that deer were a nuisance to budding shrubs. Shrubs never registered very high on the personality meter for me, so nuisance-by-deer was not a deal breaker. However, she never said one word about bears. Oh, sure, we knew about the bears in the Smoky Mountains, but nobody gave us a heads up about the beasts trotting west on I 40 to Fairlawn Glen. I would have voted against spending our senior years running for our lives from hulking, walking rugs. She also neglected to say anything about snapping turtles the size of check-in baggage either. I'll give her a pass on the Canadian geese. We saw them, we just didn't realize they were intent on taking over the country. Canada is a big country with plenty of sky. Why these silly geese insist on zooming around the United States in V formations like they own the place is beyond me. The Glen, as we transplanted locals call it, is overrun with the honking, pooping bullies. There was an article in our little newspaper about the overpopulation of geese. Apparently a roundup and relocation of Canadian geese is planned for the near future. You'd better believe I'm going to have my lawn chair set up to watch them lasso those flapping suckers.

In comparison to Michigan, Tennessee has lovely weather. Michigan has two seasons: summer (three months) and winter (nine months). If there is a spring at all, it's pretty much over in about two weeks. Autumn doesn't even last that long. I feel sorry for grass in Michigan. The spring sunshine encourages the seeds to sprout and poke their little seedling noggins skyward only to have two to four inches of snow come out of nowhere, and…*FWUMP*…grass 0, snow 1.

We settled in the Glen, a retirement/resort town known for its golf courses (we have five), golf tournaments, and anything else remotely related to golf. We also have eleven man-made lakes, and fishing is almost as big a deal as golf. There are also social clubs that play every card game ever invented, a big tennis crowd, an art gallery, walking trails, and a lot of wine tasting, bourbon tasting, gin tasting, if-it-contains-alcohol-we're-going-to-taste-it tasting.

The police don't carry Breathalyzer gizmos—if the wind is right, they can tell from forty feet whether a person is over the legal limit.

Tom was an avid golfer. In fact, he dropped dead on the golf course five years ago. Tom was not frightened to death by a bear but had a sudden, massive heart attack that dropped him on the thirteenth hole. His golf buddies said that one minute he was lining up his shot and the next he was part of the landscape, with the personality of a shrub.

My best friend, Belinda, told me about *the bear*. People throughout the Glen had started snapping pictures of the bear. Photographs began popping up in the two local newsy-papers of the bear mangling bird feeders and pawing through garbage. He didn't look all that threatening, just a "little-guy" bear. Then we learned that it wasn't always the same bear. The *bear* turned out to be bears plural. Fairlawn Glen was infested with black bears. Belinda claims that infested is too strong a term for the situation. I say, more than one little-guy bear is an infestation. Once I learned of the predator infestation, I started carrying that wasp spray stuff whenever I walk my ten-pound Maltese-and-something-else dog. Riff-Raff is four years old, and I rescued her from a seriously old lady who was keeping her in a hall bathroom. I've had

Riff for two years, and she is one of my two constant companions. My other companion is my best friend, Belinda. Belinda is a highly intelligent woman, even though she is a little naive when it comes to the very real threat of encountering a bear while walking something the size of earmuffs.

Belinda is very tall, and I am very short. She is a brunette, and I am blond (now). We know we are an unlikely pair due to the differences in our heights and personalities, but we share a strange mind/heart connection. We not only finish each other's sentences, but we start them as well. We don't always agree with each other's sentences, but we enjoy our conversations anyway.

Although Belinda and I have kept a watchful eye all summer, we've seen nary a bear. I've been hallucinating rambling bears everywhere, but so far they have all been false alarms. According to Mrs. Towers, our eighty-five-year-old, well-informed neighbor, Evelyn Lancaster in Unit 18 saw *the bear* on her patio, slurping hummingbird syrup like moonshine. She didn't get a photograph though. Knowing Evelyn Lancaster, she may have accidentally double dosed herself, and the entire alleged bear episode was an arthritis-medicine-fueled hallucination.

I normally take Riff with me everywhere in the Glen…except for the grocery store. Grocery store people are fussy about fur any place near their produce. I had to leave Riff home today, however, because I was accompanying Belinda to a funeral parlor. I didn't want to go, but Belinda pulled the "you are my best friend" card. You know the one: "I went with you when you were having your colonoscopy; the least you can do is accompany me to Marjorie's funeral." I hate that one.

Marjorie was one of Belinda's fellow Methodist church goers, and she died. I didn't know Marjorie Vickers at all really…only to share a table with her at the church Thanksgiving dinner. I didn't even care all that much for Marjorie. Marjorie's weight was very impressive. I recall that she complained before, during, and after the dinner about how awful the food was as she proceeded to inhale everything except the furniture. If the chairs had been sprinkled with powdered sugar, she might have given them a snort or two. Marjorie's excess weight probably played a role in her eventual state of deadness. You can't haul around that much fat and expect to get away with it for very long.

The viewing was scheduled for 1:00 P.M. at Walton's Funeral Home and Cemetery in the town of Clifton. Clifton is a thirty-minute drive. The Glen doesn't boast any funeral parlors or cemeteries because old people do not want to have death staring them in the face all the time. So Walton's is a frequently frequented funeral parlor and cemetery in the nearby town of Clifton. Belinda and I were not staying for the burial itself as it would likely be depressing…and hot. I am always hot. When I went through menopause, I had hot, hotter, and hottest flashes; and none of them were of the *dry* variety. Marjorie chose late summer for her life-exit, and in all this Tennessee heat there would probably be a lot of bees buzzing around the grave plot, what with all the flowers and stuff. I hate bees. Especially since the stupid things look like flying Volkswagens in the South: huge, behemoth, fuzzy bees that crowd out the sun as they fly overhead. I also detest those black wasps with the long, droopy legs that hover in place like black-op helicopters. I can outrun any bee or wasp in Tennessee, but it's easier when I avoid places they tend to frequent…like outside.

So, Belinda and I went to Marjorie's viewing all dressed appropriately and everything. I even wore my black Keds tennis shoes in deference to Marjorie's current inanimate state. I figured we would stay about fifteen minutes and be on our way to more stimulating pursuits. Maybe stop at that Chinese place in town.

The frigid air-conditioning of the funeral parlor smacked me upside the face as we left the humid Tennessee summer outside. I cannot breathe in funeral homes. It just doesn't seem respectful. Plus, the air in those places is always so thick and heavy that it feels as if you're walking through syrup. The entire funeral home environment is majorly creepy. I'm a sign-the-guest-register/out funeral attendee. I don't pace up and down making sweet noises over the flowers and everything. I don't gawk at the dead body either…and never, never, never, ever stick around for the burial.

Belinda made the appropriate viewing circuit beside the large mahogany casket while I signed the visitors' book and waited impatiently beside the exit. Mahogany is a heavy wood. Considering Marjorie's bulk, pine might have been a more considerate choice, between the mahogany, and Marjorie, I feared for the lives of the pallbearers. When you look at a funeral home viewing in its totality, the entire event is macabre and boring. There was a cluster of younger folks who I pegged as grandchildren. One girl of about fourteen wore dark, raccoon eye makeup and red, garish lipstick. A boy, perhaps a little bit older, hung with raccoon girl but didn't look too happy about it. One very well-nourished older teen bore a strong resemblance to Marjorie's older daughter, Madeline. The three grandchildren didn't wander far from one another…strength in numbers I guess. A very thin young woman caught my eye. She stood apart from an overly plump woman who was weeping while in the arms of a man of similar bulk. I recognized the woman as Marjorie's younger daughter, Audrey. I had met Marjorie's daughters at a memorial service held in Marjorie's honor at the church a few days earlier…which was another reason I was against this funeral home viewing trip: I found it to be redundant. I had been told that Marjorie also had a son, but he had been unable to attend the memorial service or the funeral. He had instead sent his wife and children. The wife chatted with Madeline and Belinda as the three of them hovered over the open casket. As I said before, majorly creepy, especially with that faint ethereal music that is a staple at these affairs.

I pegged raccoon girl, and the sullen boy, as belonging to Marjorie's absent son. None of the grandchildren had been at the memorial service. The skinny girl looked to be in her late teens or early twenties; I assumed she was a grandchild but was unsure as to whom she belonged. She stood by herself looking forlorn and bored silly. I have a healthy curiosity and a talent for keen observation.

Belinda continued to chat with the mournful family, and I could no longer stand still, so I decided to wander about the premises. Tom used to call this my "snoop mode." I slipped out to the lobby and almost collided with a thirty-something man who was standing around the corner from the doorway to the viewing room.

I caught my breath in surprise and skipped around the man. "Oh, sorry. Didn't see you there."

The man acknowledged my comment with a nod, and I drifted through the vast, long lobby that reminded me of the wings on an airplane. When I glanced back at the man in the doorway, he was peering around the corner. I got the impression that he was watching the aloof thin girl. He wasn't dressed for funeral going, but he wasn't grubby either, just very casual with blue jeans and a maroon-colored t-shirt. He held a blue baseball cap crumpled in one hand.

I shook off my curiosity. Belinda and I are notorious conspiracy theorists. We enjoy making great piles of stuff out of absolutely nothing. Our friends and neighbors have to admit that we had been right about our neighbor's death by turtle, although the actual cause of death was more likely due to the giant bonk he took to the back of the head. Still, if it hadn't been for me and Belinda, nobody would have ever learned the truth behind poor old eighty-nine-year-old Abner Cummings' death.

I strolled leisurely down the lobby area, peaking into various empty viewing rooms. Not all of them were totally empty, however. The third one I poked my head into was without funeral-viewing people, but there was a closed silver casket on a raised dais-thing at the front of the room. My curiosity got the better of me, and I drifted into the room, closing the door quietly behind me. I stepped lively (no pun intended) to the front of the room and decided to have a look-see. I couldn't get the stupid thing open and decided to abandon all efforts at identifying the mystery funeral home occupant that nobody cared enough about to show up. I looked for a guest register to sign but couldn't find one, so I left the room.

It appeared that Marjorie's was the only popular, scheduled perfor-mance of the afternoon. I continued down the long open lobby to an exit door. I was wondering what purpose the independent structure that stood directly behind the funeral home served when a man's voice startled me. "May I help you, ma'am?"

I turned around with a gasp. I do that a lot. I startle easily and inhale at the drop of a Kleenex, like an extra in a horror movie hoping to be noticed by the director. I suppose I was a little unnerved after my snoop attempt of a few minutes earlier. A nicely suited elderly man stood a few feet away with a polite funeral home director smile on his face. All funeral home directors have that enigmatic smile plastered on a smooth-skinned face. It's like they have a press-on face or something.

"Hello, sir. I am just killing…that is…wasting…that is, I'm just waiting for my friend to finish chatting with Marjorie Vickers' family."

"I see." He smiled that enigmatic smile that suggests he is the only one in the place who knows the joke's punch line.

I pointed over his shoulder in the direction of the room with the lonely occupant. "Who is the other viewing for?"

"We don't have anybody scheduled this afternoon aside from Mrs. Vickers." he answered somberly. That's another characteristic that funeral home directors share: a somber voice to go along with the press-on face and enigmatic smile.

"There's a coffin in that room back there, but it is closed. What's it doing in there if there isn't anybody inside it?"

There was a very faint sparkle in his eye. "Oh, that casket. Yes, that casket is there for display. We have a family coming in later to look at it."

"Display?"

"Yes, a family has selected that style casket for their loved one, and are coming by to make the final arrangements."

"So...nobody is in there right now? In the casket, I mean."

"No, ma'am. The family wanted to set up the casket and get a feel for the room."

Oh boy, that's rich.

"I see...sort of a trial run before the main event."

"Yes, ma'am, I suppose you could call it that." I detected the hint of a grin.

"What is that building for out there?" I flapped my hand in the direction of the separate structure.

"Oh, that's our showroom. We have our various caskets on display in there."

"Showroom? You mean like at a car dealership? Do people really do that? Come in here and pick out caskets?"

"Of course, how else would we match a specific casket with a specific customer?"

"I never thought much about it. I never volunteered to make arrangements for either of my parents. I always reasoned that one vehicle was as good as another since they all ended up in the same place. I mean, it isn't really like picking out a car, because a car you have to live with for a while, but a casket...um...well, never mind." I was babbling, "Still, I suppose that isn't a fair thing to dump on one's siblings though."

He gave a somber shake of his somber head. "No, ma'am."

Who the heck does this guy think he is, passing judgment on me like this?

"So, do the same people who pick the casket get to pick out the background music?" I flapped my hand again in the air.

"Yes, ma'am."

"You probably don't get many requests for Bob Seger or Tom Petty, huh?"

This time I was sure the grin was genuine. "Some...but not nearly as often as I would like."

This guy is flirting with me. I am being flirted with by a funeral home director. This is a first. You know, behind that plastic face and somber routine, he is kind of cute.

Fortunately I didn't have to do the whole picking out a casket thing when Tom died. He and I had discussed it all well in advance and had agreed on cremation. Unfortunately, we never discussed what we wanted done with our ashes following the...um...process. So, until I can figure out what to do with him, Tom is in a box in my closet next to my red Keds tennis shoes and my black Indigo pumps.

I looked past the man's shoulder to see Belinda walking toward me through the lobby. "There is my friend now."

The funeral home director's press-on face was back. "Good-bye, ma'am, and I am sorry for your loss."

"My loss? Oh, you mean Marjorie. Yes, Marjorie, well...thank you."

I hurried down the lobby to meet Belinda. As we passed Marjorie's viewing room, I noticed that the casually dressed man was no longer standing in the doorway. I poked my head inside the viewing room. I didn't see the thin, young woman anywhere either.

"Come on, Leslie; I don't want to attend the burial," Belinda announced as she approached.

I joined my friend at the double exit doors. "Heck, no. I have no intention of sticking around for that. It might be quite a procession though. How many pallbearers do you think they will need to haul Marjorie's remains to her final resting place? That casket looks like it must weigh a ton. Hey, that funeral home director was flirting with me back there."

"Oh, Leslie, try to be sensitive of the feelings of others, will you? These people are grieving."

"Hey, I'm sensitive! I'm so sensitive that I tried to attend a viewing in one of the other rooms, but as it turned out, there wasn't a body in the casket. The family was just doing a practice run, you know, getting a *feel* for the overall ambiance of the place. I guess they wanted to make sure the casket didn't overwhelm the room. It is a pretty big casket, but I don't think it overwhelmed anything."

Belinda stared at me in horror. "You opened a casket?"

"No, of course not."

"Well, thank God."

"I couldn't get it open."

Chapter Two

As I maneuvered down the driveway to Rivers Street, I clicked my acrylic nails against the steering wheel. I had driven to the funeral parlor in my white Kia Soul. I like my edgy, boxy little Kia. Belinda rarely drives my car. She did chauffeur me home from my colonoscopy, however, as I was still a bit woozy. While she whirred and clicked the seat and mirrors to suit her tallness, I battled the excess flatulence that is an unfortunate side effect of the procedure.

"Stop clicking your fingernails, Les. What's wrong? You always play with your fingernails when you are worried. Did that upset you back there? I know you don't enjoy funerals."

"Who enjoys funerals? I didn't get the impression that anybody back there was having a particularly good time, especially those kids. It's mean to make kids go to funerals."

I do tend to click my acrylic nails when I am deep in thought. I love acrylic fingernails. I have had them for years. They are attractive and hard as tenpenny nails. It is like having little screwdrivers on the tips of your fingers.

In answer to Belinda's query I said, "Nothing is wrong, Belinda. Not really. I was just thinking about Marjorie's family and friends. I signed the guest registry, and I didn't see a lot of your church members listed there."

"Marjorie was a good person, basically, but she could be a little bit abrasive. And she complained a lot about everything. Plus, most of the church members attended the memorial service at the church."

"Well, I went to that service. You know, Belinda, you're only going to get so much mileage out of that colonoscopy."

A few minutes later I asked, "What did Marjorie die from? She was really young. What was she, seventy-five or so?"

"Seventy-four, and she had diabetes and a bunch of other things—congestive heart failure for one. I believe the actual cause of death was a myocardial infarction."

"A what?"

"A heart attack, Les. She had a major heart attack."

"Oh, like Tom…but unlike Tom, Marjorie was lugging around an extra three hundred pounds."

"Would you please stop harping about Marjorie's obese remains? The woman had an eating disorder, all right? Sheesh, Leslie."

"Sorry. I was just thinking out loud."

"Yeah, well, you ought to have that looked at. Every thought that crosses your cerebral cortex should not necessarily fall out of your face. Get an MRI, or a CAT scan, or a lobotomy, or something!"

"Don't pretend with me, Belinda Honeycutt. I've heard you make wisecracks about Marjorie's weight too, you know. You told me one time that you sat behind her during a service, and you distinctly heard the pew creak…'like the bow of a ship,' I believe is the way you phrased it."

"Okay…okay I admit to having said some unkind things in the past. But the woman has died, Les; try to have a little respect."

"I'll try…but it isn't my fault the woman was so fat."

• • •

We split up when we got back to the Glen and went to our respective townhomes to change out of our funereal attire. Riff greeted me at the door like I was Amelia Earhart. Social outings are a chore for me. I'm a little on the antisocial side; that is, I don't much like people. I know it sounds strange for a retired social worker to admit that she doesn't like people, but you see, that was a job and, therefore, entirely different. Don't get me wrong. I *care* about people in general, I just don't *like* most of them individually. I assumed that Belinda was still annoyed by my candor, because I didn't hear from her for the rest of the day. She can be sanctimonious at times.

Belinda called me the next morning around ten. "Leslie, I have some unfortunate news. You know Roy Conklin, don't you? We are having a prayer service tonight at the church for Roy and his family. Since you know Roy, you may want to come."

"Why are you praying for Roy? What's wrong with him?" I remembered Roy from his golf outings with Tom.

"Roy's nephew, Eric, is lost in the Idahoan wilderness."

"Idahoan? Where in the heck is Idahoan?"

"Idaho, Leslie, the state of Idaho. Eric is lost in the wilderness in Idaho."

"What are you talking about? Idaho doesn't have wilderness, for heaven's sake. Idaho has potato farms."

"Well, that's true. Idaho does have potato farms, but Idaho also has miles and miles of untamed wilderness."

"I'm sorry, but I have never heard anything about Idaho having a wilderness. Alaska? Yes. Alaska has wilderness. Borneo probably has wilderness, but Idaho? Seriously?"

"Obviously your knowledge of geography is less than complete."

"Okay, answer this; assuming there is this wilderness in Idaho, how did this Eric guy get lost out there?"

"Roy said his nephew is a trained survivalist. That means…"

"I know what a survivalist is, Belinda. Those are people who store gallons of water, cans of tuna fish, and jars of peanut butter just in case there is some major catastrophe and they are the last people left on

Earth. Why would one of those survivalist types wander around in the wilderness with their stash of survival supplies?"

Belinda sighed. "Leslie, Roy's nephew is the kind of survivalist who is trained to survive out in the…well, the wilderness. Sort of like a super Boy Scout. He was supposed to check in at the ranger station two weeks ago, but he never showed up. Roy said the poor guy's wife is worried to death!"

I don't have much patience for this sort of thing, but I tried. "So, this Eric guy went out into this wilderness that you claim exists in Idaho, alone, depending solely on his wily survival training: starting a fire by knocking two stones together, building a shelter out of pinecones, stuff like that?"

"Well…yes. I guess if you put it like that. Don't you see how dangerous that would be, Leslie. Going out there alone like that? The poor guy could have been attacked by a mountain lion or a bear or something!"

"Mountain lions and bears live in the wilderness, Belinda. People are supposed to live in houses. If a mountain lion or a bear attacked this man, it certainly isn't the fault of the lion or the bear. Now, if a lion or a bear attacks my mailman right here in civilization, that would be a matter for concern. That being said, this is the United States of America. In America it isn't against the law to have a stupid hobby. If he is a good survivalist, then he will survive. I wouldn't worry too much about it if I were you."

She must have gotten annoyed with me again, because I didn't hear from her for the rest of the day. I can't get worked up over daredevils who deliberately put themselves in harm's way and then expect the rest of us to get all upset when they get hurt, or die, or get lost in the Idahoan wilderness. Nobody told Mr. Potato Head to go wandering around out there without so much as a cell phone. I do not understand those daredevil people. Some people deliberately climb up rock cliffs.

Imagine clamoring up some sheer rock wall, just because. God brings mankind all this way with roads and everything, and some guy tries to scale a rock wall like Spider-Man. God must be up there shaking his head at those idiots. To make matters worse, whenever one of these Spider-Man-wanna-bes does fall, a bunch more humans go foolishly rappelling up and down the mountain in search of him, thereby endangering even more lives. I say: hooray for America and your right to your stupid hobby, but if you go plummeting to your death, so be it. Good luck explaining that one to God.

Chapter Three

It being Sunday, I went to eleven o'clock mass and had barely returned home when Belinda *yoo-hooed* her way through the front doorway. Riff started *riff-riff-riffing*, and Belinda bent at the waist and one-handed her without even breaking stride.

"Hi, Belinda, did they find Roy's nephew? Want some coffee, or a Diet Coke?"

"Who? Oh, yeah, no, I haven't heard any more about him. Guess what I learned at church this morning?"

I sat down at the kitchen table with my bottle of Diet Coke, "Get yourself some Coke and tell me about it."

She kissed Riff on the top of her head and gave her a soft toss to the floor as she leaned into the refrigerator. Unscrewing the cap, she sat opposite me at the table, leaning in. "Marjorie's granddaughter is missing."

"Really? Missing? How is she missing? Which one?"

"The little skinny girl, at the viewing. She left yesterday morning to go back to school—she attends the University of Tennessee in Knoxville, you know, UT—and she never arrived at her dorm!"

"Yes, I do remember that girl. I felt kind of sorry for her. I got the impression that she wasn't close to Marjorie…or the rest of the family for that matter. She stood off by herself and looked bored with the entire affair." Riff was sitting on my foot, so I plopped her on my lap.

"She's Audrey's stepdaughter."

"Which one is Audrey again?"

She gave an impatient snort. "You met Audrey, Marjorie's younger daughter. Her husband and his daughter were at the viewing. Anyway, Audrey married Katrina's father two years ago, and the man's daughter was part of the deal. So I suppose that makes Katrina Marjorie's step-granddaughter."

"Katrina? Like the hurricane?"

"Well, yes, but this Katrina is about twenty, so she was born before Hurricane Katrina."

"Who told you Katrina was missing, and what did they tell you exactly?"

"Marjorie's daughter Madeline stayed behind to wrap up her mother's estate, and she was at church this morning. According to Madeline, Katrina planned to stop by the cemetery to visit her grandmother's grave before heading back to the campus, but she never arrived." Belinda finished with an ominous flourish.

"She never arrived at the cemetery?"

"No, no, at the dorm. She never arrived at her dorm."

"Did anybody see her at the cemetery? What about her car? Did her car turn up anywhere?"

"How should I know? I only heard about this after the church service this morning. Poor Audrey and her husband must be so worried about her. According to Madeline, the girl has been kind of difficult, you know, partying instead of studying; and she has a reputation for"— Belinda whispered—"promiscuity."

"According to Madeline?"

"Yes. Katrina's father has already filed a missing person's report, and the TBI is investigating, according to Madeline."

"Who are the TBI? Are they like the FBI?"

"I guess so. TBI stands for Tennessee Bureau of Investigation. That's about all I know." She frowned prettily. "I've never heard of the TBI before, have you?"

"No, but I'm going to look them up on Wikipedia. Those Wikipedia people know just about everything. What does Mrs. Towers say about all this?" Mrs. Towers also attends the Methodist church and stays up to date on all things remotely related to the Glen and its residents. She is our version of Wikipedia.

"Mrs. Towers told me to tell you about this right away. Ever since that mess with Abner, she seems to think you're Sherlock Holmes or something. It's silly really. I mean, what could you possibly do about a missing girl?"

I deposited Riff onto the floor. "Let's get my laptop, Dr. Watson, and go look them up."

Belinda and I researched the TBI on Wikipedia. Basically, they *are* the state version of the FBI. They do have a cool slogan: That guilt shall not escape nor innocence suffer. They keep crime statistics and go after methamphetamine druggies and stuff like that. Apparently they also investigate when people go missing.

"I felt an affinity for that girl, Belinda. She looked so sad, and even sadder was the apparent lack of inclusion by the family, as if she was an outcast."

"I didn't notice that, but I do remember seeing her. She was a pretty little skinny brunette. Audrey has only been married to Katrina's father for two years, and the girl was already eighteen when they married. I suppose it isn't all that strange that the girl hadn't really bonded with the family. She has been off at college ever since the wedding."

"But she was at Marjorie's funeral. Why would she be at Marjorie's funeral if she didn't give a flip about her recently acquired grandmother?"

"Probably because Audrey wanted her there, and Katrina didn't want to disappoint her stepmother or her father since she is already in trouble for partying and letting her grades slip. Audrey is the histrionic daughter."

"Ah, yes, she was the one wailing and carrying on. She made sure that she was noticed." I drummed my tenpenny nails on the table, sounding like sleet against a window. "You know, Belinda, when I left the viewing room to snoop around, there was a man watching Katrina from the doorway."

"All right, Les, don't start imagining things now."

"No, I'm serious. He was thirty-something and casually dressed in blue jeans, and carried a ball cap. He wasn't dressed for a funeral. Then when I joined you at the exit, he was gone, and so was Katrina. Or, at least I didn't see her in the viewing room, and I checked." Riff was sitting on my foot again so I picked her up. "Something about that girl and the way that man was looking at her made me uncomfortable. Do you recall seeing Katrina when you got ready to leave?"

"No, but then I wasn't looking for her either. I was actually coming to find you. You don't seriously believe that that man did something to Katrina, do you?" Her eyes widened. I couldn't tell if it was fear or anticipation. Perhaps both.

"I need to take Riff for a walk. Do you want to come? We can stop by Mrs. Towers' place and bring her up to date."

"Bring her up to date on what? We haven't done anything."

"Oh, but we have. We have my observations and a possible suspect. Are you coming?"

I changed into my blue Keds, snapped Riff on her retractable leash, and picked up my wasp spray stuff.

"Leslie, that wasp spray is not going to chase off a bear. It will probably just make it mad."

"Hey, this is great stuff! I can hit a spider from across the room. Bears are a lot bigger than spiders, Belinda. I'm pretty sure I could hit one.

Riff wouldn't stand a chance against a bear. I worry about her getting carried off by a hawk or one of those Harry Potter owls. She doesn't weigh more than a skinny rabbit."

"You have a point about the hawks, Leslie, and maybe even the owls; but I don't think you have a lot to worry about when it comes to bears. You are in more danger of having a deer crash through your windshield than encountering a bear."

"Thanks for that, Belinda. I feel all reassured now."

"No, I'm serious. You've been jumping at shadows all summer. If you did encounter a bear, though, I'm not sure that wasp stuff would deter it."

"Sure it would; one good blast of this stuff, and a bear would be blinded. Then I would grab Riff, take off, and run in a zigzag pattern so it would have a hard time following us."

"You run zigzag to avoid getting hit by bullets, Leslie, not to evade bears."

"How do you know?"

"I watch movies."

I sniffed. "I'm sure it would be just as effective during a bear chase as it is dodging bullets. The bear would be all bleary-eyed and slobbery and everything, to the point where it wouldn't be able to get a bead on us zigging and zagging."

"Well, good luck with that, Leslie."

I live in Unit number 2 and Belinda in 5. Abner Cummings used to live in number 6. I get sad every time I look at the For Sale sign in Abner's front window. We walked the length of our twenty townhomes until came to number 19, where our eighty-five-year-old widowed gossip hound resides. I rapped on the door, and we *yoo-hooed* our way into the foyer.

"Hi, girls!" Mrs. Towers sang, and I heard the creaking shuffle of our friend making her way across the carpeted living room. The poor lady broke her hip last year and has been on a walker ever since. She has one of those "Help, I've fallen etc." gizmos that old people are supposed to wear around their necks. Unfortunately Mrs. Towers fell in the bathroom, and her gizmo was on the TV tray in her living room. I can't say too much about Mrs. Towers and her wandering help gizmo. I can spend an entire day just searching for my reading glasses, and I have about fourteen pairs of them.

Belinda and I have managed to escape The Dreaded Walker thus far, although she does have one in her closet that her husband, Frank, used toward the end there…when we were waiting for him to die from his booze-soaked organs. I don't yet own a walker, as I've been fairly healthy since retirement at the age of sixty, and Tom had the good sense to drop dead without costing Medicare a fortune in health care paraphernalia. I had a lot of stuff go wrong with my body throughout my forties…including corrective surgery to both feet. I had to walk around on Frankenstein shoes for weeks. I'm good now though. I have one creaky knee, but I had X-rays, and the doctor said that I have arthritis and an old knee. I pointed out that both of my knees are the same age and only one of them clicks and carries on, but the doctor was not impressed with my keen observation. My creaky knee doesn't perform tricks. You've heard of people who have a trick knee. You know, they'll be walking along just fine and then all of a sudden one knee decides to start break dancing. Funny, you never hear about people having a trick hip or a trick elbow.

We followed Mrs. Towers and her stumping walker to the kitchen. "Get yourself some iced tea from the fridge, girls." She lowered herself onto a chair at the kitchen table. "Hand Riff up to me, Leslie, before she sits on my foot. I see you've got your wasp spray. Nobody has seen that scrawny little bear around here except Evelyn. I had my doubts about Evelyn's alleged sighting until I saw the mangled bird feeder with my own eyes. That hummingbird syrupy stuff was all over her patio.

I'll bet she has ants now like crazy." She *tsked*. "If people would stop putting out all that food for the birds, the bears would go back into the woods."

"Bears?" I asked. "You said bears, plural. How can you be sure there is more than one bear? All the pictures in the papers look pretty much like the same little-guy bear."

"Of course there is more than one bear, Leslie. After all, the Glen is a big place. If all those pictures are of the same bear, then he's been one busy little bear. And little-guy bears grow into big-guy bears."

Belinda interrupted. "Mrs. Towers, Leslie is seeing bears in her sleep as it is. Perhaps we should talk about something else. For instance, where is your help gizmo?"

With Riff comfortably nestled between her knees in the puddle of her dress, she admitted, "I don't know. I'm sure it is around here somewhere. I need a help gizmo to find my help gizmo." She cackled. "Did Belinda tell you about this missing girl, Leslie? What do you think? It doesn't sound very good to me. I am interested to hear your theories."

Belinda did an over-the-top eye roll, but I know Belinda. She is just as intrigued with the situation as I am. I brought Mrs. Towers' up to date on my observations of the day of Marjorie's viewing.

"I see," she murmured with a soft hand grazing Riff's fur. "You have a keen eye and a detective's nose, Leslie; that's for sure. So you believe that man was watching Katrina. That's an interesting development. I called over at Marjorie's when I got home from church to see whether I could speak with Audrey. She has already gone home! Can you imagine? Here her daughter goes missing, and the woman leaves this morning for Chicago!"

"Stepdaughter," I corrected.

"What?"

"Katrina is Audrey's stepdaughter. Is her father still around?"

"Oh, I don't know. I didn't think to ask."

"What about her car, Mrs. Towers? Do you know whether her car has turned up anywhere?"

"No, I didn't ask."

Belinda and I gave each other knowing glances. Mrs. Towers is a skilled gossip, but not much on the investigative front.

"Do you have any theories about what is going on with Mrs. Farrow in Unit seven, Leslie?"

"Oh, Mrs. Towers, please don't encourage Leslie's flights of fancy." Belinda groaned.

The curious activity at Unit seven *is* kind of bizarre. Several times a day, every day, package after package is delivered to Mrs. Farrow's front door by UPS and Federal Express. This maelstrom of deliveries is quite perplexing, and it's only normal for us—Mrs. Towers and me—to wonder about it. Belinda wonders too, but she refuses to admit it. Mrs. Farrow gets large boxes, small boxes, and every size in between. It is very curious.

"I've got a few theories about that, Mrs. Towers, but this Katrina thing is taking priority right now."

Chapter Four

We didn't stay at Mrs. Towers' place for long. We didn't want her to become overtired; plus, her place is a knickknack nightmare. Stupid little snow globes and porcelain/ceramic doodads cover every surface. She even has one of those collectible spoon displays hanging on her kitchen wall. There's probably a thimble collection somewhere on the premises.

I start to go squirrelly surrounded by all that *stuff*. I believe I have PTSD (Post-Traumatic Stress Disorder) as a result of my mother's ceramic period. Mom discovered ceramics, and all we heard about for months was stuff about glazes, and firing, and kilns. Soon we had ceramic frogs, rabbits, turtles, you-name-it; Mom *ceramiced* it. Christmas holidays were a dust-filled disaster of Nativity scenes and Christmas trees everywhere. I still have boxes of that crap.

I don't have knickknacky stuff anywhere in my house. I don't even display photographs of my family. I know what my family members look like; therefore, I feel no compulsion to scatter pictures of them everywhere. If I ever break a hip, it won't be because I tripped over one of my mother's stupid ceramic frogs.

As we strolled home I kept the wasp spray stuff in hand with one finger on the trigger, and we discussed where to go from here. "We should go down to the Safety Department, Belinda. Maybe Chief Braddock has some information on the missing girl."

"It's Sunday, Les. Nobody will be there."

"Darn it! I can't just sit around until tomorrow to do something. A girl's life may be in danger." I flinched. "Oh my God, what is that?"

"What?"

I pointed a shaky finger. "Oh, never mind, false alarm. It's just Larry Conroy's dog. See, there's Larry on the other end of the leash."

"You're going to give yourself a myocardial infarction! Either that or you're going to take us both out with that wasp spray stuff!"

"Aha! A heart attack. A myocardial infarction is a heart attack, and you say I never listen to you."

"True. As I was saying before your myocardial infarction episode, we'll go to the Safety Department tomorrow. There's a memorial service tonight at the church at seven o'clock for Marjorie. I'm picking up Mrs. Towers. Why don't you come with us?"

"You already had a memorial service for Marjorie. I know, because you made me go with you. And you made me go with you to the funeral home because you played the colonoscopy card. How many send-offs does Marjorie get anyway? I'm tired of saying good-bye to Marjorie. I barely knew the woman!"

"The family will be leaving the Glen soon, and the church family wants to surround them with our love…especially in light of Katrina's disappearance."

"That was a good question, Belinda, about the car, I mean."

"I have my moments."

For Katrina's sake, I agreed to accompany my friends to yet *another* memorial event for Marjorie. I was looking forward to pumping Katrina's father for clues that might point to the girl's whereabouts. I had to submit to riding in the backseat of the Riviera, *and* I had to leave my dog at home. I hoped the gathering of useful information from Katrina's relatives would outweigh these unpleasant constraints.

According to Belinda, her stupid Riviera is a luxury sports car and did not come in a four-door sedan. I made a lot of huffing and groaning noises before I finally sat back and buckled the seat belt. "I hate this car, Belinda."

"I know."

Mrs. Towers' walker was collapsed and fit neatly in the trunk. I wasn't really surprised that it fit back there; you could probably bowl in that car—it's that big.

I sat respectfully through the service, even though it was pretty boring. Since Madeline was the only one of Marjorie's children still in town, all mournful speaking fell to her. Madeline dutifully trudged to the podium and blubbered on about how much she was going to miss her mother. She recounted stories about all the wonderful times she and her sister had growing up. She didn't mention her brother except to say how much he loved Marjorie's meat loaf. Marjorie must have been a culinary genius, because it seemed like every other memory reminded Madeline of food.

I felt sorry for the three teenage grandchildren who were led to the platform and made to stand around like grieving props at a cheap playhouse while Madeline droned on and on about birthday cakes and prom dresses and miscellaneous other drivel. Then the minister started praying, and we were there for another ten minutes. The Methodists aren't one of the more energetic churches, but they do seem to enjoy praying. I know, because I grew up Methodist and converted to Catholicism when I married Tom. I was highly motivated to trade out religions. As a kid, I thought our church was the most boring place in the entire world. I spent my childhood in Flint, Michigan. We were the only Methodist family on the entire street. Everyone else on the street belonged to St. Agnes Catholic Church. My parents were almost embarrassed that they only had four children while their neighbors had virtually litters of kids.

I was envious of my Catholic neighborhood friends. Catholics seemed to have all the cool stuff. Where they had pretty rosary beads, graceful statues, special water, and candles galore, all we had were hymnals and Bibles. The Catholics even had a man who was in charge of all the other Catholics, and he lived in a palace in Rome, Italy. Our minister lived in a house right next to the church. It was just an okay house too.

When the praying started, my eyes wandered around the small congregation, and my brain starting talking to itself for entertainment.

Oh my God, Lois Stanley is wearing a wig. She was at Marjorie's last memorial service. What...she expects us to believe her hair has grown five inches in the last few days?

Boy, this church needs to do something about those broken seals on the windows. Those windows look like crap.

I'll bet Marjorie's daughter-in-law is pissed that she had to drag the kids here for her husband's mother's multiple send-offs. Yup, she's bored. She is looking at those broken seals on the windows.

I ended the conversation with myself when everybody started singing "Amazing Grace," a hymn that I used to like before it got hijacked as some kind of national anthem for dead people. When the service was finally over, the ladies of the church had a reception with cookies and stuff. I cornered Madeline to ask about her niece.

"We haven't heard from Katrina at all. Maybe she just decided to drive right out of the family." Madeline sniffed.

"I understand that she was planning to stop by her grandmother's grave before continuing on to college...." I let the sentence dangle.

Madeline rewarded me with an unladylike snort. "That's what she told my sister. Audrey has only been married to Michael for two years. It isn't like Katrina had a warm-and-fuzzy relationship with our mother. Mother hardly knew the girl. Quite frankly, I was surprised that Katrina even showed up for the funeral. She probably knew Audrey would raise holy heck if she didn't. After all, the Glen is only an hour's drive from Knoxville."

"I understand your sister has already returned to Chicago. Why is that? Isn't she concerned that something may have happened to Katrina? Is your brother-in-law still here? I met him at Marjorie's viewing, and I don't see him here tonight."

"Michael didn't want to come tonight. Like Katrina, he barely knew my mother. He is planning to leave for home tomorrow after he meets with the authorities. Audrey had to get back to her job. The world cannot come to a standstill just because Katrina has decided to pull some kind of stunt. Mark my words—nothing will come of this. Katrina is just a spoiled brat."

Madeline looked past me and called to her daughter, "Natalie, you've had enough cake. Excuse me, Leslie. I swear that girl would be as big as a house if I didn't keep after her."

I made an effort to speak with the three grandchildren, but since the funeral had been the one-and-only time any of them had laid eyes on Katrina, none of them knew anything about her. I was fascinated by the young girl in the raccoon eye make up, and I asked her if she was part of the goth culture. I learned about the goth culture from that quirky forensic character on *NCIS*. I like that show. Mark Harmon is a cutie-pie. The girl informed me that she was not goth but emo.

"What is nemo?"

"NOT NEMO...E-E-E-MO." She growled through gritted teeth.

"What is that, like Cyndi Lauper?"

When she gave me a blank look, asking, "Who's Cyndi Lauper?" I deduced that the child did not have any useful information to offer.

I grabbed a cookie and wandered over to eavesdrop on Mrs. Towers, who was having an animated conversation with someone. I did an about-face when I recognized the other end of the conversation. It was

Roy Conklin, the uncle of the doomed survivalist, and I didn't want to get into *that* again. Sadly, it wasn't a permanent reprieve.

I had to listen to Mrs. Towers, and Belinda's lamentations about Roy's nephew the whole way back to our complex. I did manage to keep my opinions to myself this time. We muscled her walker from the trunk, got Mrs. Towers into her house, then motored down to number five. I shut the passenger door on Belinda's U-boat-size vehicle with a mighty heave, complaining, "Well, that was a waste of time. We didn't learn anything at all." Startling Belinda, I let loose a furious "$#!+ !"

"What? What's wrong?"

"We forgot to ask about the girl's car. We need to know whether that car has been discovered anywhere. We don't even know *what* she was driving. I can't believe we wasted an entire evening."

My friend unlocked her door, and I trooped into the house behind her. "It wasn't wasted, Les. You said that the girl's father is leaving tomorrow, and Madeline doesn't seem to be all that worried about her niece either. Maybe it is a stunt. Maybe she is paying her parents back for forcing her to attend the funeral. Maybe she just wants to cause them a little worry?"

"Perhaps…but I have an uneasy feeling that she's not in a very good place tonight. Did you know that Marjorie's funeral is the first time any of those grandchildren had even laid eyes on Katrina? And, what about that little girl who looks like Darth Vader ran over Tinker Bell? I asked her who she was pretending to be, and she started talking about some bizarre culture."

Belinda laughed. "What about her? Aw, come on, Leslie. Don't tell me you never wanted to emulate a movie star or singer when you were a teenager."

"I wanted to be Cher; but I was too short, and I couldn't sing."

"You could have been Sonny."

That was pretty funny.

Chapter Five

Monday morning at 10:30 Belinda and I were on our way to the Safety Department to see Quinn Braddock, the safety chief in the Glen. Fairlawn Glen is not incorporated, so we don't have a regular police department. The police department and the fire department share quarters at the Department of Public Safety. Quinn is a veteran of the Tennessee state police and a good-looking devil. Belinda thinks he resembles Leslie Nielsen…when Leslie Nielsen was alive, that is. "We can't be too obvious about how we go about this, Belinda. We have to be discreet."

"I will be the soul of discretion, Leslie. It's you I worry about."

"Ha! I've got the perfect cover. We will tell Quinn that we are following up on those mailbox hooligans. That happened a while ago. He owes us a report."

I was referring to the night three weeks earlier when three kids went whooping down our street, and bashing mailboxes in our complex. It was around 10:00 P.M. when Riff jumped off the sofa and started running back and forth to the front door like a chipmunk with a personality disorder. When Riff has to go potty after dark, she usually doesn't go much beyond the front porch before hitching her rear end over the grass while keeping her front paws on the sidewalk. Riff doesn't like to walk on wet grass, and I can't say that I can blame her. The sprinkling system for the townhome complex pumps water directly from the lake; Tom thought it was genius, as it saved on the water bill. I'm not so sure that I want lake water spewing all over my lawn. I mean, who knows where that water has been? Or what or who has been *in* it?

Since all summer every shadow was a potential grizzly bear, I flipped on the porch light and whispered, "Hurry up, Riff. Watch out for the bears." I was shocked when I opened the front door and Riff went barreling through the door, *BOW WOW WOWING* across the front lawn, totally oblivious to the wet grass. She was just a white streak in the darkness, racing toward the street, which was dimly illuminated by carriage lamps attached to the mailboxes. Wearing what I call my flannel "clown pants" and a faded Detroit Tigers' sweatshirt that I have had for close to forty years, I stepped onto the porch calling Riff. Distant growling sounds reached my ears, and I soon realized this was the growl of engines and not bears. The sound grew to a roar descending on Lake Manchester Townhomes.

Then I saw them. Headlights attached to four-wheeled vehicles bouncing through the entrance. Three really fast, dark, loud blurs flew past my unit. I went running after Riff in my slippered feet right through the lake-soaked grass. I heard the whooping and hollering of teenage boys and then *BANG…CLANG…CRASH.* Carriage lamps went dark all along the complex streets.

I ran flat-out, yelling at the top of my lungs, "YOU GET OUT OF HERE, YOU SONS OF B!+@#%'$. YOU BETTER NOT HURT MY DOG!" My husband worked at Pontiac Motors and taught me how to swear and mean it. The kids wheeled around and came ripping back down the road toward the complex entrance. I had made it to poor old Abner's driveway when I saw Riff coming at me like a flying squirrel.

"Oh, Riff." I sat down right in the middle of the driveway, and she jumped into my lap. I was crying into her fur when porch lights started going on up and down the street. Belinda rushed to where I was sitting.

"Oh, Leslie, honey, what happened? Are you all right?" She helped me to my feet, and I went into the house with her, blubbering into Riff's fur. A bunch of neighbors called 911, and members of the Safety Department showed up. I was mortified to have to give my story clad in clown pants, a threadbare sweatshirt, and lake water-soaked slippers. I'm a little bit too seasoned to be tangling with teenage thugs in the middle of the night.

"You're right." Belinda said. "We never heard whether they caught those kids, did we? I suppose it wouldn't hurt if we went down to the station and spoke with Chief Braddock."

"Yes, and I will discreetly work in a question or two about Katrina without arousing suspicion. Somehow we need to get him to give up what he knows about Katrina's car."

Belinda grumbled her way into the passenger seat of my Kia Soul. "I do not understand why you insist on driving around in this ice cream truck."

"Oh, shut up. I didn't bellyache last night, even though I was wedged like Gumby in the back of your stupid Riviera." There are two things that Belinda's late husband bought for her that she refuses to part with—one is a 1998 Buick Riviera, and the other is her long-haired cat, Butter. Butter is allegedly half-feral, the result of a pedigree Persian female and a mystery man-cat. I've never seen anything remotely wild about Butter. Maybe one day he will go all "feral" on us, but so far he resembles a big, long-haired sofa cushion.

Riff vaulted into the car, scrambled in front of me, and landed in Belinda's lap. Once positioned in the cockpit with my seat belt fastened, I cautioned my friend, "Now, remember that we need to approach the situation discreetly, Belinda. I suggest you follow my lead."

Belinda muttered loud enough to make sure I could hear, "Yeah, because we all know how you're the *soul* of discretion."

Before exiting the vehicle, Belinda and I checked our faces in our respective car visor mirrors. I wear my blond hair in a chin-length bob...sort of a modern-day version of Doris Day. Belinda's style isn't that much different from mine, except her hair is a luxurious chestnut brown. Only our hairdressers know for sure.

"I think we should split up." I suggested as we entered the building.

"I'll go see if there are any Wanted posters," she whispered before gliding nonchalantly toward the bulletin board.

The tops of two heads were visible above the partial wall divider that separates the open lobby area from the offices. The offices are cubicles separated from one another with more partial wall dividers. It's a pretty flimsy setup. A table sits snugly against the wall divider between the lobby and office areas. The table contains pamphlets and stuff related to the Glen: boating rules and whatnot. The boating rules are pretty much a joke. They just go on and on in detail about the "No Wake" restriction in all Fairlawn Glen lakes. *"No Wake" means maintaining a speed of no greater than 5 miles per hour, or such as is necessary to maintain steerage and headway, so that there is no white water in the path of the boat or in waves immediate to the boat.* In other words, you cannot leave so much as a fart-bubble behind your boat.

I heard a rumble of male voices and the higher-pitched voice of a woman. I assumed the male voices belonged to the floating heads. The woman's head was evidently too short to float.

I pretended to be engrossed in some of the flyers on the table, straining to make out words. I thought I heard Chief Braddock say "Walton's," but I couldn't be sure. I couldn't get any closer to the wall without climbing on top of the table—which would have been indiscreet. I thought about scooting Riff around the side of the wall, thereby giving me an excuse to go in after her, but I figured the three of them would stop talking the minute they saw me. Carrying Riff, I hurried over to where Belinda stood examining notices on the board.

"Belinda," I said in a soft voice.

"Hmmmmm?" she answered distractedly. "Did you know the Wilsons are selling their pontoon boat?"

Oh, good heavens! Belinda is looking at the For Sale stuff. "Belinda," I whispered more forcefully.

"What?" she asked in her normal Belinda voice.

"Shhhhh! Lower your voice."

"What?" She mimed the question in an exaggerated fashion.

"You're taller than I am," I whispered.

She responded in an exaggerated stage whisper, "Oh, my word, Leslie, do you mean that you haven't been aware of the disparities in our respective heights until this very moment?"

I rolled my eyes and continued to whisper, "Two men and a woman are talking over there by the wall. I think one of the men is Chief Braddock, and I believe I heard him say something about Walton's. Go over and see if you can hear what they are saying."

Without speaking, Belinda made the "okay" sign with her fingers.

We traded places. Belinda moseyed over to the table, and I began to peruse the bulletin board. I didn't find any Wanted posters but noticed the Wilsons are indeed trying to sell their boat.

I glanced furtively in Belinda's direction every few seconds. Suddenly the talking heads started to bob along the wall top, and Chief Braddock and another male officer walked into the lobby through the open space that served as a doorway, an illusion created where the divider stopped and the wall opposite it began. A woman with shoulder-length dark-blond hair followed them through the improvised doorway. She wore minimal makeup and no jewelry except for some pearl-looking button earrings. She was slim, taller than I am—but then almost everybody is—wearing slacks, a blazer, and a button-down blouse open at the collar.

Belinda pretended interest in a brochure but sang out when Quinn came around the partial wall divider. "Hello, Quinn! It's so good to see you. My friend Leslie"—she pointed in my direction— "and I thought we'd stop by to see whether you've caught the mailbox hooligans. Neither of us will feel safe until they are behind bars." She finished dramatically. My friend struggles with subtlety.

All three of them stopped at Belinda's greeting, and I hurried to join my (not-so) subtle friend. The woman smiled at both of us, then turned toward Quinn. "Thank you for your time, Chief. I'll be on my way."

Not so fast, lady.

I juggled Riff into my other arm and hopped in front of the lady to thrust my hand out at her to shake. "Hi, my name is Leslie Barrett, and this is my friend Belinda Honeycutt." I trilled the introduction as though she should be just tickled to death to meet us.

The woman shook my hand. "Hello, ladies, it is nice to meet both of you."

When she didn't say anything more, I asked bluntly, "And you are?"

"Leslie, don't be rude," Belinda scolded, and then stepped forward just as bold as brass, shaking the woman's hand. "I'm sorry, I didn't catch your name."

I fought back a smile. Belinda's lack of subtlety is effective at times.

Quinn cleared his throat and said, "Ladies, this is Agent Hailey Donnelly. She is with the Tennessee Bureau of Investigation."

"Oh, the TBI," I gushed. "Yes...yes...we are familiar with the TBI, aren't we, Belinda? I imagine you're here about the missing girl, Katrina?"

"Uh...well," the agent stammered, "yes, actually, I was just touching base with the chief here about Katrina Stephens. He was telling me about Walton's and the cemetery."

I nodded, delighted that I had been able to ferret out the girl's last name so effortlessly. For some reason it had escaped my notice last evening…along with details about Katrina's car. I wasn't going to let that happen again. "Belinda and I saw her, you know…Katrina…we were at the viewing for her grandmother. Marjorie was a dear friend of mine." As I made the claim, Belinda's eyes practically clacked as they rolled in her head.

"Have you spoken with Katrina's father? I understand that her mother…were you aware that Audrey is Katrina's stepmother and not her mother…anyway, Audrey has already returned to Chicago." I looked at Agent Donnelly expectantly.

Quinn interrupted, "Mrs. Barrett, Mrs. Honeycutt, Agent Donnelly is looking into this matter for the Stephens family. I will let her know how to get in touch with you should she have any questions for you." This guy was giving us the bum's rush, but I wasn't ready to have my bum rushed.

"What were you telling Agent Donnelly about the cemetery, Quinn? What's there to say, other than give her directions maybe?" I persisted.

"The Clifton police have had some reports come in about lights flickering throughout the cemetery. Several of the neighbors across Rivers Street have called in sightings," he explained.

"What do you mean? Do they suspect our mailbox hooligans are riding around in the cemetery? There hasn't been any vandalism, has there?"

"No, no vandalism. Forget I mentioned it. It's probably just some kids creeping around the cemetery with flashlights, trying to scare themselves. There is no connection to the missing girl."

"We understand that Katrina was planning to stop at Marjorie's grave on her way back to UT. I found that a little bit strange; after all, Marjorie was only the girl's step-grandmother, and it was clear to Belinda and me that Katrina wasn't very close to her." I raised my eyebrows.

Agent Donnelly opened her mouth as though in dismissal but seemed to think better of it, asking, "What makes you say that? I did know that

Mrs. Vickers is the girl's step-grandmother, but why do you assume the two of them weren't close?"

Belinda popped out with "Body language…Katrina's body language just screamed 'boredom.'"

"And," I jumped in, "she stood by herself, apart from all the other family members, almost like they were shunning her, or her, them."

"Thank you, ladies for sharing your observations with us." Now she *was* dismissive. "I have to be going. It was nice meeting you both." She nodded her head at Quinn, and he nodded back.

As she started to walk by me, I raised my voice to inquire, "Did anybody see the girl's car at the cemetery? What was she driving again…?"

Agent Donnelly stuttered in her step as she admitted, "A Kia…a red Kia. One of the small ones."

I leaned toward her. "A Rio? Or a Forte maybe? Kia makes some very good cars, you know."

"A-a Rio, I believe." She frowned severely. "I must be going, ladies. I wouldn't worry about the girl too much. According to her parents, she has done this before."

I rose on my tiptoes. "Done what before? Disappear, you mean?"

"I'm sure it isn't as serious as you make it sound, Mrs. Barrett. The girl has gone off before without letting her parents know where she was going. After all, the girl is twenty years old."

Belinda practically barked, "*Katrina*, the *girl's name is Katrina*. The poor *girl* may have been kidnapped!"

"Or murdered," I interjected, nodding fiercely in support of my indignant friend. Belinda is a very sensitive person.

Belinda mimicked my nodding and harrumphed, "Yes, kidnapped or murdered, for all we know. Your attitude seems rather cavalier, Agent."

Agent Donnelly grimaced and announced emphatically, "Good-bye, ladies." She started toward the exit, but I called after her, "Agent,

Agent," and she stopped, heaved a big sigh and turned toward me. "*WHAT?*"

"You forgot to give us your business card. If we remember anything else about Katrina and the day of the viewing, we will need to get in touch with you. Also you never did say whether or not Katrina's car has been found."

Agent Donnelly gave a sniffy harrumph of her own. "No, I didn't, and if you remember anything, let Chief Braddock know. He can get in touch with me."

I shook my head. "No, that won't do, I'm afraid. My friend is right. This young woman's life may be in danger. Surely you don't want to waste time playing phone tag. You'll want to follow up on clues immediately in order to bring the poor child home safely."

She sighed again, stuck a hand in her pocket, and held out a card with two fingers.

I snatched the card. "Thank you, Agent Donnelly. If we have any further information for you, I promise we will keep you informed."

"Yes, well, good-bye." She walked swiftly to the exit and hurried through the doors as if she was scared I was going to take her down like a stray antelope.

Belinda and I made our good-byes to Quinn and the other officer and hurried from the building. I was dying to interrogate Belinda about what she may have heard over the top of the wall divider.

Once buckled into her seat, Belinda complimented, "That was slick how you worked in the part about Katrina's car. I thought that agent was pretty snooty not to answer your question."

"Thanks, Belinda, but cops often withhold information from the public. What did you overhear?"

"I was only able to catch a word here and there, Les."

I keep a writing tablet in my car. One never knows when one may need to copy down a license plate number or something. I twisted between the bucket seats and plopped the tablet in Belinda's lap with the mechanical pencil I keep clipped to the cover. "Okay, tell me the words you heard and write them down while I drive home."

"I did catch the name *Walton* a few times." Belinda started to write.

"I knew it. What else?"

"In addition to *Walton*, Quinn said *cemetery*."

"I knew it!" I squealed. "What else?"

"I might get the words out of order, but I definitely heard the other officer say the word, *spray*."

"*Spray*? Really? Oh God, Belinda! I'll bet he was referring to arterial spray! You know, like when an artery is severed, and blood sprays all over the place!"

"Watch out for the squirrel, Leslie!"

"I saw him. I missed him. Well, I'm pretty sure I missed him."

After that Belinda made me wait until we were inside my kitchen before she would tell me any more.

I handed Belinda a Diet Coke, and we took our seats at my kitchen table. Riff nosed around in her food dish and then moseyed over to sit on my foot.

"Okay, Leslie, I know that Quinn said *Walton's* a couple of times and *cemetery*. The other guy said *spray*, and, Leslie, you cannot assume he was talking about arterial spray. That's a lot of blood to have been overlooked. Anyway, the other man said *vase*."

"*Vase*?" I interrupted. "He probably said *face*, Belinda. You know how that arterial spray is; it would have gotten all over the killer's face and his clothes. Maybe he said *clothes*."

"He said *vase*, Leslie. *Clothes* doesn't sound at all like *vase*."

"Okay, okay, maybe he said *face*?"

Belinda acknowledged that it was possible he had said *face*. "That's all I can remember."

"You couldn't hear anything being said by Agent Donnelly?" Riff whined, and I picked her up.

"No, she had a soft voice. All I could tell was that it was a woman doing the talking."

"Let's review what we do know. We know they were talking about the Walton place and a cemetery. Walton's cemetery covers a lot of acreage."

"Yes, Walton's cemetery must cover at least ten acres." Belinda nodded and sipped.

"We know what kind of car Katrina was driving and the color, and we know that Katrina was being watched by that man."

"That was just your impression, Leslie. You have no proof that the man was watching Katrina. In fact, Agent Donnelly was probably correct. Katrina just went off to visit some friends for a few days and neglected to tell her parents. You said yourself that Madeline wasn't all that concerned."

"No, Belinda, something has happened to Katrina. I can sense it. Katrina was standing there and that man was watching her and then, suddenly, they were both gone! I feel certain that she met up with that man."

"So what? She is a twenty-year-old woman, after all, and we know that she didn't leave Marjorie's house until the next morning."

"Exactly!" I trumpeted. "So she could stop by her dear, departed step-grandmother's grave to pay her respects on her way out of town. The step-grandmother that she didn't give one hoot about! I believe she met up with that man again…and then…"

"What? Then what, Leslie? He murdered Katrina?" She flapped her arms. "Why do you always have to be so melodramatic? Everything with you has to be about murder or government espionage or something.

You really need to sign up for Ancestry.com. I bet if you explore your genealogy, you'll discover you're related to Lizzie Borden! Your family probably had to change their name to Barrett to escape the stigma."

"Barrett is my married name, Belinda. My maiden name was Honcoop."

"All right then, research Honcoop. I wouldn't be surprised if the original gang was Bonnie, Clyde, *and Selma Honcoop*!"

"I cannot help the fact that I have an innate talent for snooping. So, sue me if I am concerned about the fate of this girl. I am simply trying to follow the tracks left by the perp. This is no different from what we did when we found Abner's killer."

"Those two men were never charged with Abner's murder, Leslie. They…"

"Yeah, I know, I know; they claimed it was an accident and that all they did was throw poor old Abner's dead body into the lake to be carted off by humongous snapping turtles. I told you how big that creature was that I saw crossing the road shortly after Tom and I moved here. Besides, Abner was in that lake for so long that any forensic evidence that would have pointed to murder…"

"All right, Leslie, that's enough. I do *not* want to go over all that again. The entire episode was horrifying! Poor Abner. He was my neighbor, you know."

"Well, he was my neighbor too, and don't pretend that you didn't have as much fun as I did. The way you handled that boat was nothing short of spectacular! You were waking up a tsunami!"

Belinda slurped her Coke, trying to hide a grin…and failing.

I set my empty bottle on the table forcefully. "We should go over to Walton's and look around."

"Look around for what?"

"Clues, of course! See whether anything hinky is going on out there."

"Describe *hinky*."

"Oh, Belinda, stop being difficult. We should go for the purpose of determining whether anything looks suspicious. Maybe find out the identity of that man who was watching Katrina. See whether we can find her car anywhere."

Chapter Six

I made a couple of quick grilled cheese sandwiches for lunch. I slid Belinda's sandwich onto her plate and walked back to the stove.

"Want any pickles?"

"No, thanks."

"Olives?"

"No, thanks."

"Potato chips?"

"Yes, please."

"Too bad, because I don't have any." Grinning, I handed Belinda the bag of potato chips.

After lunch we headed out—again in my Soul. Belinda and Riff rode shotgun. I pulled into the long drive leading to the funeral home. It's a one-way, looping drive with stone grave markers lining each side like parade watchers. The cemetery borders Rivers Street for at least five acres on either side of the entrance. Small houses dot the street facing the cemetery.

I parked in the funeral home lot, tossed Riff to the pavement, and climbed out after her. "I don't see any-body around, Belinda. Monday must not be a big day for cemetery visiting. I'm going to check out that building behind the funeral home."

"What do you suppose is in that building?" she whispered nervously, falling into step beside me. "You should put Riff on her leash."

"Nobody is here. Riff will be okay. She never goes too far from me.

And why are you whispering? It isn't like anybody out here is going to hear you."

"Respect, Leslie. I'm trying to maintain some measure of respect."

As we walked, in a normal voice I told Belinda, "The funeral home director told me that that building is their showroom...you know, where they stack the caskets and people mosey around and pick out a preferred vehicle for their loved one's last journey."

I didn't have a big-deal funeral for Tom. I didn't feel like Tom would have liked me to put on a show for him. I did allow the Catholic church to hold a memorial service, but that was it. Tom has been in my closet ever since. I got some flack about not arranging a separate memorial service for Tom in Michigan so that our miscellaneous siblings and Tom's General Motors' friends there could pay their last respects. I told them to go ahead and have a service if that is what they needed to do. As far as I was concerned, we had a lovely memorial service at our local church, and everybody in Michigan who wanted to attend had been invited. Other than our daughter, Carrie, and our granddaughter, Janie, nobody showed up. Even Carrie's husband, "What's-His-Name," didn't come down for Tom's memorial. I can't say that I blame him though. Tom and I barely acknowledged his existence except for some socks at Christmas. Carrie isn't all that fond of the man either.

Belinda was gracious about the entire funeral hoopla when Frank died two years ago. She was very accommodating to everyone. There was a tasteful memorial at the Methodist church (which I attended) and then Belinda schlepped Frank and his coffin back to Philadelphia, where her two sons were planning a showy send-off for their father. I stayed here and looked after Butter. Evidently Frank had once been a successful, big-deal prosecutor out in Philadelphia before he retired and drank himself to death. It was probably wise of Belinda not to go the route of cremation. Seeing as how Scotch-soaked Frank's body was, he might have gone up like a natural gas explosion.

The showroom was a separate building directly behind the actual funeral home. A gravel lane ran between the two structures. I approached the entrance and noted a sign next to the door that simply said, CASKET DISPLAYS. I tried to open the doors.

"What are you doing?" Belinda asked in her regular Belinda voice.

"What does it look like I'm doing? The door's locked. Katrina could be trapped in there."

"Oh dear God, Leslie, you can't be serious!"

"Maybe we can get the funeral home director guy to let us look around. He really liked me, Belinda. I could tell. He was flirting with me."

"What are you going to say to him, Leslie? 'Hi there, cutie-pie, remember me? How about we take a stroll through your casket farm?' What? Don't you think he'll find it a little suspicious when you start lifting lids?"

"I told you already. I can't lift the lids on those things, but I do see your point. Still, I would like to get a look in that building. Katrina could be lying on the floor in there, unconscious, or tied up!"

There was at least fifteen feet of well-tended lawn on all three sides of the building, providing a respectful grass moat between the structure and the plotted graves. Starting at the entrance, I walked the face of the small building and turned down the right side, intending to walk its circumference. An assortment of lawn care equipment leaned against the side of the building. A few shovels, rakes, a wheelbarrow, a kid's wagon, and several small buckets. One bucket had a bunch of small rocks in it. I have no idea what for. It seemed odd—a bucketful of rocks.

"What are we doing now, Leslie?"

"We are scoping out the place."

"Scoping?"

"Yes, scoping. You know, looking around. Who knows? Katrina's little red Kia could be parked here or something."

We walked around the entire structure and found nothing. I wandered back to the rear of the structure again with my two companions at my heels.

"All scoped and no car," Belinda announced. "Why are we still here?"

Riff was having a great time with all the new things to sniff. The only windows in the entire place were in the back and were at least a good six feet from the ground. Not even Belinda would be able to see through those windows.

Some shabby-looking headstones were leaning up against the building. "I wonder why these are here?"

"Maybe they haven't had a chance to put them up yet. Leslie, why are we standing around back here? This is dumb."

I ignored her. "No, these look really old." I picked up one of the smaller ones. "Oh, Belinda, look. This is the headstone for some little kid. How sad is that?" I scrubbed at the date of death on the headstone. "I can't tell what year little Stella Marlowe died. It's worn off, 1920—something. Poor little thing."

Riff barked, and Belinda shrieked a strangled, "Oh God, Leslie. Someone is coming...A man, is that the man? Let's run. Oh God, Leslie-e-e-e!"

I scanned the immediate area. There was indeed someone coming. A fit-looking man walked toward us from the depths of the graveyard with a long-handled rake in his hand. He was indeed the man who had been watching Katrina at Marjorie's viewing. As he got closer, I could see that he was a good-looking young man. Katrina may very well have taken a shine to him.

"What...huh, huh...what...huh, huh?" Belinda was doing a bunny hop.

"I've got an idea," I said under my breath, then yelled, "*YOO-HOO!*

Young man! *YOO-HOO!*"

"Jesus Christ, Leslie, he could be a kidnapper, or a killer. What in the world?" She was back to whispering, but it came out like she was being strangled.

"Trust me." I strode confidently into the cemetery, weaving around headstones to greet the man. Riff was at my heels, but Belinda stood cowering against the building.

The man narrowed his eyes and asked, "What are you ladies doing back here?" He didn't sound at all menacing, just mildly curious, and he didn't appear to recognize me.

"My friend and I do headstone rubbings. We noticed these"—I hefted the small stone for emphasis—"leaning against the building. The year of this poor soul's death is completely worn away."

"Yes, ma'am, I know. Those markers are back here because they need restoration work. We have a volunteer group that takes care of that for us. Why would you be interested in these markers? Obviously there are many to choose from in the cemetery." He waved an arm casually to indicate the surrounding acreage.

"We noticed these small stone markers back here and were curious. Maybe we could borrow this one of little Stella Marlowe to complete a rubbing. We have everything we need in my little truck. I see that you are carrying a rake. Do you work on the grounds, Mr....?" I left the question dangling in the hopes that he would fill in his name.

He didn't offer up his name, but he did admit, "Yes, ma'am, I work in grounds maintenance. And"—he frowned—"I also try to keep an eye out for security purposes."

I babbled, "I can see that you don't want us back here. That is quite all right, young man. We will do a rubbing on a stone still standing. Thank you very much. You have been very helpful."

Riff whined and put her front feet smack on the man's boot, looking up at him with a yearning on her little face. He squatted down and sat on his haunches long enough to give her a scratch behind one ear. He stood with a slight grunt and reached for the small grave marker. "I'll take that, ma'am."

"What?" I realized I was still cradling the little girl's headstone and promptly handed it over. "Thank you again, young man."

Turning, I sang to Belinda, "Come along, dear," but she had already taken off toward the car. Riff was still staring up at the young man, and I had to cluck at her to break whatever spell she was under.

I swept Riff up in one arm and jogged to catch up with Belinda. "Slow down, Belinda; walk normally. We have to make a show of looking at other tombstones."

"Oh God," she whimpered, "was that him?"

"Yes, that is the man that I observed watching Katrina." I knelt beside a couple of headstones as though considering their potential for rubbings.

"I don't believe that nice young man had anything to do with Katrina's disappearance."

Regaining my feet, I lectured, "I know that you value your bull meter, but you may be off on this one. He could be a sociopath, Belinda. A sociopath is totally devoid of feelings."

"I know what a sociopath is, Leslie, and that man was too polite to be a sociopath. Look at how warmly he responded to Riff."

"Yes, well, Ted Bundy was a polite young man too. A polite, young, sociopathic man."

"Well, I think you are wrong. Riff would have detected something if the guy was a nut."

"Belinda, we both know that Riff would slobber all over Satan if she thought there was an ear rub in her near future."

We climbed in the Soul, and I hit the automatic door locks.

"You locked the doors!" Belinda shrieked. "You think he's a psychopath!" She swiveled her head to look back the way we had come. "Is he following us?"

"A sociopath," I corrected my best friend. "No, he isn't following, but he is watching."

"Let's get out of here, Leslie. We might make him suspicious. Do you think he recognized you?"

"I'm pretty sure he didn't recognize me. I bumped into him in the doorway on the day of Marjorie's viewing, but there was nothing remarkable about it. I'm only taking precautions by locking the doors," I reassured my friend. I often rely on my social work background when situations become emotionally charged. Belinda is excitable at times.

We both watched as the man went around the side of the building and reappeared near the casket showroom entrance no longer carrying the rake.

"Look." I pointed my finger so that Belinda twisted around in her seat to peer in the direction I was pointing. "He's leaving."

The man was walking away from the showroom toward a small pickup truck. He climbed in the truck and drove down the long drive and turned onto the street.

"It's close to one o'clock, maybe he's going to lunch?"

I quickly unlocked the doors. "Come on; we probably have at least a half hour."

"Leslie, I think we should just go home." Riff jumped from my lap, and I slammed the car door.

Riff and I were already headed around the back of the showroom building. I stood looking up at the window as Belinda rounded the corner to join us, grousing, "Now what are we doing? We already determined that the car isn't back here, Les."

"Here, link your fingers and boost me up to the window."

"No. I'm liable to throw out my back. Why don't *you* boost *me* up?"

"Look around for something we can stand on; wait a minute." I ran off, returning with a small, stout bucket. Dumping the rocks onto the ground, I flipped the bucket over and placed it against the wall directly beneath the window. The bucket looked like it would give us at least another ten inches or so. Planting my hand on Belinda's shoulder, I stepped onto the bucket. No good. I was too short. The top of my head still didn't reach the windowsill.

I looked down at Belinda with pleading eyes. "Oh, get down," she complained. "You watch to see if that guy comes back." With that, Belinda clambered onto the bucket, cupped her eyes with her hands, and placed her forehead against the glass.

"See anything? Caskets and stuff?"

She glared down at me. "No, Leslie. I do not see any caskets and stuff. I do not see Katrina or anybody else lying unconscious or trussed up on the floor. I do not *see* anything." Turning back to the window, she mumbled into the glass, "I'm not Batman. It is black as pitch in there."

"Bats are blind, Belinda. That is why there is the expression 'blind as a bat.'"

"Yeah, well, Batman is not blind, all right?"

"No need to get testy." I picked up a rock and handed it to her. "Here, break the window."

"Are you totally out of your mind?" she gasped. "We are not breaking into a coffin factory, for God's sake! Anyway, they probably have an alarm system."

"Don't be ridiculous. Why would they have an alarm system? Who would want to break into a casket place?"

"You, for one. So much for discretion!" Using my shoulder as leverage, she stepped down from the bucket and then clapped her hands. "Hey, here's an idea! Why don't we put my cell phone in the video mode and tie it to Riff's collar. We could bust out the window and toss Riff inside to video the premises. Then she could call us when she's done!"

I love Belinda, but she does have a sarcastic streak.

"Very funny, and it isn't a factory, Belinda. They don't make the things here; they just display them."

Belinda looked behind me. "Speaking of Riff, where is she?"

I looked around but couldn't see her.

"Riff," Belinda called in a loud whisper.

"Riff!" I hollered, and was rewarded with an answering bark. "She's over there, in the direction that man came from."

Riff was about four rows into the cemetery, and we skirted the graves to get to her.

She was digging furiously in some fresh dirt at a new grave. Picking her up, I brushed dirt from her nose. "Riff, don't run off like that."

"Oh, look, Leslie, this is Marjorie's plot. Look at all the flowers! They are fresh too. Poor Marjorie."

The grave plot was covered. There were two huge wreaths leaning up against the headstone. One said MOTHER and the other GRAND-MOTHER. Smaller, yet still good-sized arrangements lined both sides of the grave with tall gladiolas and sprigs of pussy willows. Still other bouquets contained lilacs and various other colorful flowers.

"They are beautiful, aren't they?" Belinda mused sadly. "Look, the twenty-third Psalm is engraved under her name." She began to recite the words on the stone: "Though I walk through the valley of the shadow of death, I will fear no evil."

"Yeah, I know; I love that one. We'd better get going, Belinda. That guy might come back any minute." I froze as one of the biggest bees I've ever seen in my life lifted ominously from behind the O in GRANDMOTHER. I swear it hovered for a second, staring right at me.

What a time to be without my wasp spray stuff.

With a loud yelp, I took off running. I was running up and over and through dead people, and I did not care. I could feel more than hear Riff galloping at my side, no doubt thrilled with the afternoon romp.

I was halfway to the car when my mind caught up with me. Turning, I held a hand to my side, trying to catch my breath, and saw Belinda fast-walking toward me. Whereas I had just bulldozed my way through the mob of dead people, Belinda was reverently observing the pathway.

She approached while scolding, "Good heavens, Leslie, it was just a bee. Didn't anybody ever tell you not to run when you encounter a stinging insect? The sudden movement is what causes them to chase you."

My sides were heaving. "I can't help it, Belinda. It is some kind of atavistic response to danger. You know, fight or flight. I'm not a fighter. Besides, did you see the size of that thing?"

"Are you all right, Leslie; you seem to be having trouble catching your breath."

"I'm all right."

"You are out of shape, Les. You really need to get more exercise."

"I exercise. I take line dancing classes. I went just last Tuesday."

"How often do you attend?"

"Classes are held weekly."

"How often do you attend?"

"Well, I try to go every week unless I have something else to do, or the mean lady is teaching."

"Uh-huh." Belinda is proud of her exercised self. She still attends the Wellness Center in the Glen. It's a busy place stuffed with exercise equipment and old people. People seem to love it though. I tried to love it through three memberships. I finally had to admit that I do not wish to sweat on purpose.

Now I warned, "Don't start with me again about that pool. I will not get in that pool unless I am on fire, Belinda."

I started the car and prepared to leave the premises. As I pulled onto Rivers Street, I said casually, "You really like Quinn Braddock, don't you?"

"What is that supposed to mean? Of course I like Quinn."

"No, Belinda, I mean that you *really* like Quinn."

"Don't be silly. He's a married man."

Belinda shrieked, and I almost drove off the road and into a gravestone.

"God, Belinda! Don't do that!" I reprimanded sharply. "I do not want to die in a head-on collision with a tombstone!"

She had twisted around in her seat and powered down the window, and she and Riff both stuck their heads out. "Leslie, isn't that the truck that guy was driving?"

"What guy? Where?" My head flew from side to side.

Heaving an exasperated sigh, she hauled Riff back inside the car and pointed. "The guy from the cemetery. His truck is sitting in a driveway back there. I'm sure of it."

I peered in the rear view mirror, "I don't see it."

"Turn around, Leslie. I swear it's the same truck. I'm calling 911."

Reaching across, I stayed her hand. "What are you going to tell them? Hello, 911? We just saw this creepy cemetery guy's truck, and we're pretty sure he's responsible for Katrina Stephens' disappearance because we saw him ogling her at her grandmother's funeral?"

"You have that agent's card. You could call her and tell her about him. You should have told her about him in the first place!"

I sighed. "Again, Belinda, what was I supposed to tell her? Besides, I didn't see any tape across your mouth. *You* could have told that agent just as well as I."

"*I* didn't observe the man stalking Katrina!"

I turned around in a driveway and motored slowly back down the street. The cemetery was now to our right and the row of little shabby houses to our left. Then I saw the truck.

"You know what, Belinda? I think you're right. It is the same truck. It would make sense that he would live close to his work. Maybe he goes home for lunch? I wonder why he didn't park in the garage?"

"Oh God, Leslie, you don't think he has that girl's car stashed in his garage, do you? Maybe you really should call that agent."

I continued on past the house and pulled to the curb.

"What are you doing?"

"Here is what we are going to do. You and Riff wait in the car...."

She didn't let me finish. "Oh no Leslie, you are not doing this. You cannot confront this guy alone!"

"Calm down. I'm not going to confront anyone. All I'm going to do is look around a little. I will be covert."

"Covert!" she squawked. "This isn't the CIA, Leslie! I'm calling 911."

She had her phone out again. Again I stayed her hand. "I'll be careful. You can see the house and the truck from here. If you see anything terrible, then you can call 911. Okay?"

"Define *terrible*."

"Don't be silly. I'm just going to have a little look-see in the garage."

"Okay," she answered shakily, glancing out toward the truck. "Wait a minute! He's leaving."

I looked back and noted he was indeed exiting through the front doorway. We watched him climb into his truck, back down the driveway, and drive off in the direction of the funeral home/cemetery.

"See, he's gone. I'll be fine. At least we'll know whether or not Katrina's vehicle is in that garage. If it is, I'll come back, and you can call 911, and I will call Agent Donnelly."

As I prepared to get out of the car, Belinda whispered, "For heaven's sake, Leslie, be careful."

I nodded my assent and shut the door.

Chapter Seven

I had learned from TV that the best way to go unnoticed is to act as though you belong. So I set out walking down the sidewalk as though I walked the block daily. I didn't look around suspiciously or otherwise call attention to myself.

As I approached the house where the truck had been parked, I walked confidently up the driveway. I slipped along the one-car garage on the house side, hugging the wall with my back. I didn't have to worry about being seen by anyone across the street because those people were all dead. I slunk along the wall as if I were taking tiny line dancing steps. I maneuvered silently around a wind chime that hung in the corner L where the garage met the house. It was one of those robust wind chimes: long metal tubes that clang and gong together in a strong breeze. Again, being as quiet as possible, I sidled up beside the front picture window.

Peering through a gap in the curtains, I caught a vague, shadowy movement. Something was moving low to the ground, but I couldn't tell what it was. I saw the regular room stuff: a sofa, tables, chairs, television, etc. A soft, growly *Woof* sounded deep in the house. With my back against the wall, I retraced my steps across the front of the house and walked right into the wind chime, with the metal tubes whacking me upside the head. *CLANG! CLANG! CLANG!* Followed by a deep *Woof, woof, woof."*

"Holy crapola!" I cursed under my breath.

I wrapped my arms around the stupid wind chime and hugged it to my chest, clacking my jaw in the process. With a muffled *CLUMPFFF*, it went silent. I gradually started to breathe again but ridiculously refused to open my eyes. I felt like a little kid playing You-Can't-See-Me-If-I-Can't-See-You.

When nothing happened, I carefully peeled the individual pipes from my grip until they once again hung obediently silent. I crept around the dreaded musical apparatus, walked swiftly across the driveway, and slipped around the side of the garage. I did my shuffling two-step with my back to the wall until I reached the window of the garage. I sent up a silent prayer…not sure if I was praying to find Katrina's car or not.

I turned to face the wall of the garage and ducked below the window. I did a quick pop-up-and-down preliminary glance in through the window. Then, easing my head above the windowsill, I cupped my hands around my eyes to counter the glare. No car. The garage was just full of garage stuff: lawn-mowing equipment, hobby tools hanging on a far wall, but no car. I decided to give the backyard a look-see and resumed my two-step sideways shuffle.

Just when I thought I was home free, I heard the slap of a screen door, footsteps, a child's laughter, and splashing sounds coming from the backyard.

The invisible dog *woofed* once again only to be told by an invisible (to me at least) woman, "Stay inside, Rufus." I stopped in my tracks as the sounds were coming from right around the rear corner of the garage. I went straight up in the air when unexpectedly Riff appeared at my feet. She gave a couple of yips of joy like she was the seek to my hide and then zipped around the garage and into the backyard. Thank God that big *woofing* dog was still inside the house.

"Puppy!" a child squealed with delight. "Mommy, look, a puppy!"

"Hello there, where did you come from?" A woman's warm voice.

Woof woof woof from inside the house.

"Quiet Rufus!" The woman hollered.

Yeah, be quiet Rufus…and don't eat my dog.

Belinda loped around the corner of the garage, gripping my pink Cinderella umbrella like a baseball bat. It's a dinky little plastic thing that doesn't provide protection from more than three raindrops and is definitely not robust enough for clobbering. I bought it for Janie but liked it so much that I kept it for myself.

In a soft voice she panted, "Leslie, are you okay?"

"I'm *fine*; just follow my lead." I walked past Belinda toward the front of the house, and Belinda spun to follow. I executed a perfect jazz-box maneuver that would have made my line dancing instructor proud and called, "Marshmallow, where are you, girl?" I strode past Belinda toward the backyard, and she spun around to follow.

"What are you doing?" she whispered. "You're making me dizzy."

I rounded the corner of the garage to find a little girl about three years old sitting in a small wading pool. The mother—I assumed she was the child's mother—was holding Riff. When she saw me, Riff started struggling in the woman's arms, and the woman set her on her feet.

"Marshmallow, you bad girl, come here, sweetheart," I scolded and cooed. Riff came to me immediately, and I scooped her into my arms. Belinda stepped into view around the corner of the garage.

"I'm so sorry, ma'am," I gushed, "my friend and I were taking a walk, and little Marshmallow here must have heard something and took off. I should have had her on a leash." Without another word, I turned and walked past Belinda (again), and she whirled in place and followed.

"Leslie, what are we doing?"

"Leaving."

"Why did you call Riff 'Marshmallow'?"

"I don't know. I panicked."

Walking briskly toward the car, we could hear the child wailing, "I WANT PUPPY!"

Belinda told me that she had been on pins and needles since I exited the car. She was already coming after me when she heard the wind chime racket.

"I envisioned you lying on the ground, surrounded by overturned metal garbage cans. I couldn't leave you out there all alone!"

God, how I love this woman.

"Well, you weren't going to do much damage with my Cinderella umbrella," I teased as we climbed in the car.

She pitched the Cinderella umbrella into the backseat. "Well, excuse me, but you must have left your shotgun back at the ranch. Not only that, but Marshmallow is a dumb name for a dog."

"This, coming from a woman who named her cat after margarine."

Chapter Eight

We were halfway back to the Glen when I laid out my plan of attack. "Belinda, we have to go back to that cemetery tonight. We'll park on the street near the entrance. You'll have to drive. I can't see well enough to drive at night; plus, your Riviera is black, so it won't be as noticeable as my Soul."

"Leslie, I am not going on a stakeout in a cemetery. Besides, you said Katrina's car wasn't in that guy's garage. There's every reason to believe that he is just a nice, hardworking lawn maintenance guy with a sweet wife and a darling, little girl. I'm convinced Katrina has just run off somewhere."

"That wasn't what you were saying to Agent Donnelly back at the Safety Department. You were positively passionate about how no one is taking this girl's disappearance seriously. Don't stamp this guy's forehead as normal just yet, Belinda. After one particularly riveting episode of *NCIS*, I looked up serial killers on Wikipedia. There are general characteristics cataloged for serial killers, of course, but the killers don't seem to be aware of them."

"I don't want to hear this, Leslie. I swear to God I am going to put a parental lock on your TV."

I ticked off examples on my fingers. "Number one: Serial killers have average or below average IQs—except when they have above average IQs. Number two: Serial killers have trouble staying employed and/or work menial jobs—except when they have steady jobs and sometimes they're even professionals…like Hannibal Lector, he was a psychiatrist."

"He was a movie character, Leslie, and why on earth are you memorizing statistics about serial killers?"

"Number three: Serial killers come from unstable families—except when they appear to have normal families. So you see, Belinda, our lawn maintenance guy could most definitely be a bad guy with a sweet wife and a darling little girl. He probably even loves dogs. Did I tell you I heard a dog in the house? It was a big dog too. Granted, it is likely an aberration for a serial killer to like dogs, but that butterfly killer guy in *Silence of the Lambs*, remember he had that little-bitty dog that he was crazy about?"

Belinda held her head in her hands and ground her teeth. *"That was a movie, Leslie!"*

"I know it was a movie, Belinda. But don't forget; that movie won best picture at the Academy Awards. They have stringent criteria for those awards. They couldn't just knock out some flimsy, scary movie without sound research."

Belinda sighed. "Okay, Leslie, I give up, but couldn't we call Agent Donnelly and let the TBI stake out the cemetery?"

"Belinda, they are not looking for this young woman. Not even her parents are looking for her. *No one* is looking for her. *Someone* has to care about Katrina."

"Okay, but I'm not hanging around a cemetery all night. I'll agree to a couple of hours only. What do you expect to see in the dark anyway? You just admitted that you can't see at night."

"To *drive*, Belinda. I can't see to *drive* at night. Quinn said that strange lights have been observed in the cemetery; maybe there is some kind of connection."

"So what? Dancing lights in a cemetery are probably just kids messing around. You said as much to Quinn yourself. I don't see what strange lights in the cemetery have to do with Katrina Stephens' disappearance."

"I don't believe in coincidences, Belinda. Nothing *ever* happens around here, but now we have mysterious bobbling lights hopping around a cemetery *and* Katrina Stephens vanishes after visiting her grandmother's grave at that very same cemetery. Don't you wonder about the timing of the two?"

"No. We don't even know for sure that Katrina went by the cemetery on her way out of town."

"Belinda, now, think long and hard about this next question. Do you have anything better to do tonight?" After a long, silent pause I announced, "I suspected as much. Now, we need some stuff from the store."

"Dollar General or Foodstuff City?"

Three years ago Fairlawn Glen finally got its very own big-chain grocery store. You would have thought the world's fair had come to town. We were positively giddy with excitement, as it meant we no longer had to travel *all the way* into Clifton (ten miles) for provisions.

"Dollar General," I said. "I need to pick up a flashlight for tonight. All I have is a little one. Cemeteries are probably seriously dark places."

"Wait a minute, Leslie. You have to promise me something before we take this stakeout thing any further. If we see anything…and I mean *anything*, call 911 and let the authorities take over. We are *not* leaving the car."

"I promise. I want the flashlight though, just in case."

"I mean it, Leslie. I'll be driving. You do anything dangerous, and I will haul us out of there."

"Sheesh, Belinda. I thought I was supposed to be the melodramatic one. I already promised."

"I already have a big, heavy flashlight, Les. I will bring it tonight. I probably need to pick up some batteries though."

The Dollar General Store in the Glen is always jammed. I love the place. They have tons of stuff stacked up all along the aisles, in the middle of aisles, piled up to the ceiling. As far as I'm concerned, if the Dollar General doesn't have it, I don't need it.

As we entered the store, I suggested Belinda roam around the store, and I would do the same. We each grabbed a cart and went our separate ways. We both ended up in the "As Seen on TV" aisle. All Belinda had in her cart was dish detergent and toilet paper. I had a couple of greeting cards, a big plastic flashlight, and Riff. The Dollar General people had given up objecting to Riff-Raff riding around in the child seat of the grocery cart a long time ago. A lot of people around the Glen have purse-size dogs.

"Hey, look, Leslie, here are some binoculars for nine ninety-nine. These could come in handy tonight."

"I already have binoculars, remember? Tom bought them for me after I saw that yellow finch at the golf course. He was hoping I would join the bird-watching club." I gave an unladylike snort. "Like *that* was ever going to happen. What are you supposed to do, lug those goofy-looking things around all the time? I mean, I like yellow finches, but it isn't like you spot a yellow finch and whip out binoculars like a sidearm. You should buy some though, Belinda. It's fun to watch the marina...especially when the grandchildren are in town."

From our back patios we have a great view of the Lake Manchester Marina sprawled along the opposite shore. It's a pretty lively place on holidays when the little grandchildren come to town. My grand-daughter is twenty now. Grandchildren aren't fun once they turn into people.

"No, thanks, Les, when I want to watch nothing going on at the marina, I'll borrow your binoculars."

"Ha, they came in handy when Abner..."

She cut me off with a hiss. "I do not want to talk about Abner."

"Well, fine." Belinda and I don't spend a lot of time fussing over hurt feelings.

"Those binoculars of yours are powerful though. Tell you what…I'll bring my heavy flashlight and you bring your binoculars; they might come in handy."

"Okay, but it is going to be dark. I don't know how much help the binoculars are going to be in the dark. Ooooooh, wait a minute; look what I found! I've seen these advertised on TV!" I triumphantly thumped a package into her hand.

Pursing her lips she said, "I don't know; these look like they are more for night driving than night snooping."

"Belinda, the packaging promises." I squinted, trying to make out the words. "I don't have my reading glasses; here read what this says right here." I pointed at the package.

Obediently she read aloud: "Reduces night driving glare and eye strain! HD vision! HD lens technology."

"See there…HD lens technology! Heck, for nine ninety-nine I don't see where we can go wrong. You never know; we may have to chase the suspect in the dark on the interstate. If that happens, you are going to be very glad to have these glasses."

Belinda narrowed her eyes. "*I'm* doing the driving on this escapade, and *I'm* not chasing anything in the dark on or off the interstate!"

"Well, fine. They still only cost nine ninety-nine. I'm getting a pair."

"Okay…" She sighed. "I don't see the value, but I don't see the harm either."

We each put a pair of wrap-around "As Seen on TV" night vision glasses in our carts. Riff sniffed the package and sneezed in approval.

We continued to poke down the aisle when Belinda suddenly shrieked. Reaching over the top of my head, she plucked something off the top shelf (I hate it when she does that). She held out a green, shriveled-up something in a plastic bag.

"What is it?" I asked. "It looks like a big hair scrunchie."

"It's one of those watering hoses that expands when the water shoots through it, then shrivels back up when you turn the water off." She looked down at me with one of her mischievous grins. "This reminds me of Frank."

"What?"

Grinning, she elbowed me. "You know—his what-cha-ma-call-it—his ding-dong—his weed whacker—his dilly-dally…"

By this time I was laughing so hard I was practically crying. Riff gave a little yip which only made me laugh harder.

I suppose it was no surprise that one of the clerks came to check on us. "You ladies all right?"

"Y-e-s. We're fine. Sorry," we both sort of burbled.

As I drove home, Belinda took the night vision glasses out of the package and slipped them on. "Oooooooo, Leslie, these are really cool. I'm glad you insisted we buy them. Everything has an amber tint. It's very soothing. And, look…"—she raised the glasses from her nose—"they fit right over my regular glasses."

"Let me see." I reached for the glasses.

Belinda relinquished them, and I slipped them on. "Oooooooo, you're right. These are great!" The world took on an eerie amber glow. Because they have the wrap-around feature, there were small side windows to prevent any loss of peripheral vision. Since my cataract surgeries I can see far away like Superman. Now I can see like Superman in the dark.

"Hey, give them back."

"Nuh-uh, I love these. Get out the other pair. Besides, they were my idea. Everything is so distinct. It must be the HD lens technology."

Belinda was ripping into the other package.

We agreed to meet at Belinda's at 6:30 P.M. That would allow us plenty of time to get to Walton's and get set up before it started to get dark.

"That gives us three hours, Belinda. What are we going to do for three hours?"

"I don't know. Take a nap or something."

"I've got an idea."

"I figured you would."

I want to talk to those grandchildren again…especially that raccoon girl. If anybody noticed anything suspicious going on at the viewing, it would have been that raccoon girl."

"Leslie, smearing black mascara all over your face does not heighten one's awareness."

"You don't have to come if you don't want to. Go ahead and take a nap. Riff and I will drive over to Marjorie's and take them a pie or something. When somebody dies, you are supposed to bring food to the family. I was loaded up with casseroles and stuff after Tom died. I wouldn't be surprised if there aren't still a couple in the back of the freezer."

She sighed. "I'll go with you. It would be a nice gesture to take them a pie or something. I seriously doubt those children have magical powers of observation, but we need to kill a few hours. Are you going to call over there first?"

"No. I don't want to give them a chance to say no to a visit."

Chapter Nine

We swung by Foodstuff City and picked up a store-made apple pie and then motored over to Marjorie's place. Marjorie's daughter-in-law, the woman sent by proxy to represent her husband, answered the door.

"Hi," I trilled, holding up the pie like it was an award at the Academy Awards. "I'm Leslie Barrett, and this is my friend Belinda Honeycutt. Belinda and I have been to all Marjorie's farewell events. We brought a pie over for the youngsters as a gesture of our church's...um...love. It's a Southern tradition."

The woman smiled. "How kind of you. Thank you. Yes, I do recall meeting both of you ladies. I am Louise Vickers, Todd's wife. Todd was just brokenhearted that he couldn't come to his mother's funeral, but he's an ophthalmologist and has a very busy practice in Cleveland." She winced as she said that last part.

Too busy to make time for his dead mother? Guy must be a real prince.

"That's nice. May we come in?" I took a few steps forward, eliminating any opportunity for her to refuse.

She held the door open and accepted the pie. "Of course, we're packing up to go home."

"Oh good. The pie will give the children something to look forward to when you get home. It might even cheer up your husband."

Belinda was carrying Riff and traipsed into the living room behind me, waving one of Riff's paws at Louise in passing. "This is Riff-Raff,

Leslie's dog. Riff wasn't able to attend any of the services."

I immediately sat down on the sofa. This was a ploy I learned from my days in home health. Some patients were not as welcoming as others, so I developed some effective social work techniques such as sitting down and blabbing about nonsense, or picking up a photograph (most people display photographs) and gushing something like "Oh, who is this cute little fella?" That was generally all it took to break the ice with a new patient.

Belinda dumped Riff in my lap and sat down beside me on the sofa. Louise was still standing.

I looked around and noted that Marjorie's place was crammed with knickknack crap too. It must be some sort of hoarding disorder. Thank God it isn't genetic. "Did your brother-in-law go home today?"

"Yes, Michael left right after he spoke with that lady agent."

With a puzzled frown, I suggested, "That was sort of abrupt, don't you think? I guess he must not be too worried about his daughter."

She looked uncomfortable but said, "Well, he had to get back to work...just as Audrey did. I am sure they're both very concerned about Katrina. Audrey and Michael have only been married for two years, and it isn't as if Katrina was a child when they married. She's a grown woman, after all." She seemed willing to cut Katrina, Audrey, and Michael more slack than Madeline had the previous evening. I decided that I liked Louise Vickers.

"Still, when a parent files a missing person report, it sounds pretty serious to me." I shrugged. "But, maybe that's just me! I'm sure that he knows his own child."

"Are your children around?" I was developing a very convincing trill. "We're embarrassed that we didn't greet the children properly at the services. Marjorie's death must have been very difficult for them."

"Yes, well, Mother's passing has been hard on all of us." She just stood there with that pie in her hands.

Belinda jumped in with a lifeline. "We can't stay long, Louise, especially since you're obviously getting ready to head home, but we really did want to express our sympathies to the children on behalf of the church family, you know."

"Oh, sure, of course, I'll get them. I'll just be a minute." She walked swiftly out of the cluttered-with-knickknacks room.

Riff was struggling to get down on the floor, but I held her in my lap. "Look at all this crap," I whispered.

"I'm sure it wasn't crap to Marjorie."

"Yeah, well…" I mumbled.

Louise returned with raccoon girl and her older brother in tow. Neither one looked too happy to be there. She tugged her daughter forward. "This is our daughter, Marjorie."

"Oh," Belinda burbled, "you were named after your grandmother. How nice."

"Gee," the girl said sullenly.

"Excuse me?" I shifted forward in my seat.

"Gee. Nobody calls me Marjorie." She lifted her chin defiantly.

Belinda couldn't seem to stop burbling. "I see. You go by one name, like Cher or Madonna."

"Who?" Gee frowned.

I patted Belinda on the knee. "Give it up."

The way she changed when she noticed Riff on my lap was nothing short of magical. "Oh, what a cute dog!" She plopped on the floor in a heap. "Can I see him? Please?"

"Her," I corrected. "Riff-Raff is a female." I couldn't resist grinning at the transformation from the gloomy, sullen teen to that of the delightful child she obviously was. I scanned the carpeting to reassure myself that Riff wasn't going to be contaminated by anything and set her lightly on the floor. Riff gave a couple of tentative exploratory sniffs and then launched herself at Gee.

Louise smiled down at the laughing child and met first mine and then Belinda's eyes with an appreciative twinkle. Riff was happily slurping Gee's face and I cringed. "Oh, honey, don't let her do that. That tongue has been in places that aren't talked about in polite conversation."

Gee and Riff completely ignored me.

Jeez, she's going to get that black goop all over Riff.

I had to restrain myself. The two of them were having a great time, and hearing the child giggle was worth the risk of black goop.

The boy was watching his sister as his mother introduced him. "This is our oldest, Denny."

"Dennis," he immediately corrected his mother. Louise gave a slight roll of her eyes and continued, "Kids, this is Mrs. Barrett and Mrs...."

"Honeycutt," Belinda offered. "I went to church with your grandmother."

"Kids, you'd best get back to packing up your stuff now," Louise suggested, and the kids ignored her.

As did I. "You kids must be worried about your cousin."

Gee paused in her tussling with Riff long enough to ask, "Who?"

"Katrina," Louise advised. "Uncle Michael's daughter, you know, you've met Katrina."

"Oh *her*." Gee went back to nuzzling Riff, who was practically purring from the attention.

I looked at Dennis. "So, what do *you* guys think happened to Katrina?"

He shrugged. "How should we know? We didn't even meet her until Grandma died."

"She's a slut," Gee announced.

"*Marjorie*," her mother scolded.

"Don't pretend, Mom. I heard you and Aunt Audrey talking about her. She probably just ran off with some guy. Oh, and she smokes too. Now *that* is just wrong on *so* many levels." Gee sniffed airily.

"Marjorie, that isn't nice." Louise scolded again and then added for our benefit, "Audrey told us that Katrina has been a little...um... unsettled. I'm sure the police will locate her soon."

I eyed the kids. "Did you children see anybody at your grandmother's funeral who didn't seem to belong there? Perhaps someone who showed an interest in Katrina?"

"Mrs. Barrett, I don't want the children to worry about that girl, that is, their cousin." Louise attempted to put a halt to my line of questioning.

Dennis piped up with. "There was that one guy."

Belinda and I gave each other a quick glance, and I hurriedly asked, "What guy?"

"Aunt Madeline was upset because Grandma's coffin wasn't raised up high enough, and that old man went to get some other guy to help him crank up the table some more."

"A man around thirty in blue jeans and a baseball cap?" I suggested excitedly.

Dennis frowned. "I don't much remember what he was wearing other than he wasn't dressed for church or anything." He wrinkled his nose. "He smelled like cigarette smoke. The guy helped the old man crank up the table. It wasn't easy either because they had to crank it up by hand and..."

"Dennis," his mother warned.

Dennis gave me a knowing grin. "Anyway, the guy helped raise the table and then he just left."

"Did Katrina leave the room at any time? I mean, after that guy came in to crank up the table?"

He gave an exaggerated shrug. "I don't know. I wasn't paying any attention to her."

"What about you, Gee? Did you notice whether anyone took a special interest in your cousin?"

Gee gave an exaggerated shrug. "Nope. I didn't care about Katrina. Maybe she slipped out to have a smoke and met up with that guy. Maybe she hooked up with him. After all, she was a slut."

"That's enough, Marjorie," her mother scolded. I suppressed a grin.

Louise had her hand on her throat. "You aren't implying that man had anything to do with Katrina's disappearance, are you? That isn't possible. Katrina came back here after the funeral. She didn't go anywhere until she left the next morning."

Gee was gaping at her mother. "Yeah, Mom, to go *by the cemetery...* remember? Maybe she met back up with that guy at the cemetery?"

"Enough"—Louise looked at me sternly—"all of you. Kids, go finish packing."

I clucked at Riff, and she reluctantly returned to me. I scooped her one-handed and stood. "I'm sure that Katrina will be found safe and sound. You children needn't be concerned about your cousin."

Belinda stood as well. "That's right. There's nothing to worry about. We'll be going now. Have a safe trip home, and enjoy the pie."

Louise all but threw us out the front door.

Once we were back in the Soul, I started the engine. "Gee got that black goop all over Riff's fur. I'm going to have to get out the baby shampoo when we get home."

"Who did you say she is supposed to be emulating with all that sparkly eye shadow and black mascara? What kind of skirt was she wearing? It looked like one of those tutus that ballerinas wear." She barked a laugh. "And those boots!"

"Gee is emo. And she isn't *an* emo, she *is* emo. That is (I spelled) *E-M-O*. I looked it up last night after she told me about it. Even Wikipedia has a page about it. From what I was able to gather, the culture started in the mid-1980s with punk rock—punk rock was just really terrible music with a lot of screaming—anyway, the songs were all about torchy, dark, hysterical feelings."

"In other words, kids who go all emo are just being teenagers…especially the girls."

"Exactly. They wear that dark, garish makeup and look-at-me clothing. Carrie went through a Cyndi Lauper phase. Cyndi was just kind of lighthearted and goofy in comparison to raccoon girl. Imagine, that poor child doesn't know who Cher is. I can forgive her for not knowing about Madonna, but seriously, *Cher*? I keep forgetting that this generation doesn't appreciate relevant history. If it doesn't beep, tweet, or text, they don't know anything about it. We did get some valuable information though from both Gee and Dennis."

"So what if that man and Katrina both smoked; it doesn't mean anything."

"Just as Gee suggested, maybe Katrina slipped out of the viewing room for a smoke. After all, Katrina and the man were both missing from the viewing room when we met up to leave. I had a feeling the raccoon girl, Gee, that is, would be the observant type, and I was right."

I hadn't detected the odor of cigarette smoke when I bumped into the man in the doorway of the viewing room. Tom was the one with the sensitive nose. Tom could detect a cigarette from two counties away. He said it had to do with growing up with a mother who smoked like a woodstove.

"Maybe, just maybe, this is all conjecture, Les."

"No, I really think we are on to something here."

"Of course you do."

Chapter Ten

I grabbed a short nap before I had to head to Belinda's. Once awake and ready to rumble, I rifled through my dresser drawers for appropriate stakeout clothing. I already had my night vision glasses and binoculars ready to go. All I needed was the plastic flashlight from Dollar General. I gave Riff a bowl of the good stuff for dinner. I wanted her to have sufficient energy to tackle whatever might be ahead of us. Kibble is *not* the dinner of champions.

All dressed and geared up with important places to go, I felt an uneasy twinge in the pit of my stomach. There was risk involved in the task Belinda and I had assigned ourselves. The smart thing to do was to arrange for some backup. I decided to give Agent Hailey Donnelly a heads-up on the night's planned activities, so I fished her business card from my wallet. Her cell phone went directly to voice mail. She either had it turned off or she was talking with somebody else at the time of my call, so I left the following message: "Hello, Agent Donnelly, this is Leslie Barrett. My friend Belinda and I are headed over to Walton's cemetery in Clifton. I thought I'd let you know because I don't want us running duplicitous maneuvers to those of your agents. I noticed a man watching Katrina the day of Marjorie's viewing, and today we learned that he works at the cemetery in grounds maintenance. We are going to remain on stakeout for a couple of hours after it starts to get dark. If we run into anything unexpected that leads to Katrina, we may have to call you for backup. Bye-bye." I rang off.

I was dressed entirely in black when I got to Belinda's at 6:20 P.M. I had the binoculars hanging around my neck and my night vision glasses in my pocket.

Belinda snorted a laugh when she saw me. "Why are you dressed like a ninja?"

My ensemble was as follows: a black wool knit snug cap, black t-shirt, black slacks, black socks, and my black Keds' tennis shoes. I found a black lightweight jacket of Tom's and wore that over the top of the t-shirt. While the t-shirt itself is black, there is a white-and-red blazing Chevrolet Corvette across the front of the shirt. Tom got it for me as a souvenir on one of his Pontiac Motors' sanctioned trips. Tom had to travel on occasion for his job, of course. On one arduous trip, Tom was forced to endure San Francisco, and a tour of the NUMMI (New United Motor Manufacturing Incorporated) plant in Freemont, California. He was only gone for a few days, but he had accomplished quite a bit in that short time. The newly learned engineering stuff he imparted was: trolley cars are really fun, the San Francisco Bridge is impressive, Lombard Street is exciting to drive down, and the Redwood Forest is magnificent. He brought me a t-shirt that said PROPERTY OF ALCATRAZ.

"You know, Les, you're going to sweat to death in that jacket, and I know how much you hate to sweat."

She was correct about the jacket, but it covered up the Corvette. I suggested she exchange her white BORN IN THE USA t-shirt for something darker. She came up with a brown t-shirt with yellow lettering across the front that said I LISTEN TO THE VOICES IN MY BRIEFS. She said that Frank bought it for her when he was in New York City for a professional seminar. I also made her swap out her sandals for walking shoes.

"I'm only going to be driving, Leslie."

"You never know. You don't want to have to chase anybody down wearing Jesus sandals."

"There isn't going to be any chasing."

"Humor me, Belinda; change the shoes." She grumbled but exchanged them for her walking shoes.

Butter lay on the comforter feigning interest. Riff and Butter get along quite well. Riff jumped on the bed, Butter hissed at her, and Riff jumped down. That is generally the extent of their exchanges.

Leaving Butter behind, the three of us traipsed through the garage and loaded our paraphernalia into the backseat of the Riviera. I had to nudge Riff out of the way constantly as she performed her sniff test on our stakeout gear.

Belinda settled into the driver's seat, and I passed Riff across to her. She punched the garage door opener, and as it rumbled up on the overhead chains, I complained my way into the vehicle. I fastened my seatbelt, which meant the shoulder harness laid smack across my windpipe. Groaning, I attempted to close the door—which I could not do because of the windpipe-crushing shoulder harness. Belinda snickered at my antics, which caused me to grouse that much louder. Unfastening the seatbelt, I stretched my upper body to the point where I was in danger of falling out headfirst. Grasping the door handle with both hands, I hauled the door closed with a loud, protesting grunt from me and a resulting vacuum-sucking *vrump* from the door. Refastening my seatbelt, I said, "Okay, let's roll."

"Night vision glasses, Les?"

I one-handed them from my pocket and slipped them on. Belinda was already wearing hers. We backed down the driveway to whatever awaited us at Walton's.

Chapter Eleven

It still being summer, there was a lot of daylight left when we arrived at Walton's. I suggested we drive by the casket store.

"Why?"

"To check it out."

"Check what out? We already determined we can't see through the window. Besides, somebody might see us, like that groundskeeper."

"We were in the Kia the last time we saw him. He won't recognize the Riviera. Go…"

Belinda begrudgingly obliged and cruised down the long drive toward the funeral home.

"Park along here." I pointed to the curb near Marjorie's grave. "If the groundskeeper guy comes by, he'll assume the car belongs to some of Marjorie's family."

"We are not getting out of this vehicle, Leslie. I thought I made that perfectly clear!"

"*After dark*, Belinda. I agreed to remain in the car *after dark*. It isn't dark yet." I huffed my way out of the vehicle—"Stupid freakin' car"— and dropped Riff to the pavement.

Belinda grumbled, "I don't recall any stipulation about darkness."

Riff and I followed the drive behind the funeral home. I was standing hands on hips in front of the showroom doors when Belinda trotted up beside me, not even winded. She takes such delight in showing off her exercised lungs and nonarthritic knees. "I don't see any cars in the parking lot to suggest that the funeral director or embalming people are still here. I think we are good to go, Belinda."

"Where are we going?"

Riff and I started poking around the front of the structure, lifting up rocks.

"What *are* you doing?"

"Looking for the door key, of course. Reach above the door and see whether it's hidden up there somewhere."

Riff and I started poking around along the side of the building. I picked up rocks, and Riff sniffed around bushes. Belinda called out, "Leslie!"

"What?"

"The door's unlocked."

Riff and I hurried to her side. "Hmm, I wonder why?" I frowned.

"Don't know. Let's go back to the car."

She was too late. I was already pushing the door open. I slipped inside, with Riff at my feet. "Come on, Belinda." It was very dark, but I sensed the room was large. I felt Belinda slip through the doorway and pull the door closed. *Now* she was breathing hard.

"It's pitch-black in here," I announced. "We should have brought your flash..." Riff and I both yelped when a harsh, bright light flooded the room. "What did you do?" I asked stupidly.

"I turned on the lights," Belinda replied as though I were stupid.

"Why did you do that? Somebody might see the light?"

"Unless they are ten feet tall, nobody can see through that dinky window."

"Light may leak around the doorframe."

"You're right. Let's go back to the car."

Riff sauntered off between the rows of display caskets.

"Wow, look at this place. It looks like a colony of vampires." I leaned into a shiny blue coffin with cushiony lining. My voice came out a bit muffled. "Wonder how much space they leave between the person's face and the lid when it is closed."

"Don't know. Why don't you scramble on in and I'll close the lid. It looks nice and comfy inside there." She snapped her fingers. "Oh shoot, we didn't bring a tape measure. How are you going to measure between your nose and the coffin lid?" If it was possible, she added in an even more sarcastic tone, "What's the matter? Are you worried that the occupant can't breathe once the lid is closed?"

"Very funny." I trailed my hand along the top of several of the shiny coffins, wondering aloud, "Do you suppose they give these things names? You know, like cars?"

"I don't know."

"You picked one out for Frank. What did you do, just point at one and say, 'I'd like that one in red, please.'"

"Pretty close. Except it was bronze, not red."

"Bronze? Isn't bronze third place?"

"In Olympic medals, Leslie. I'm not aware of any Olympic events that involve caskets. There isn't anything in here to interest us. Let's go back to the car."

Riff started *riffing* from the left side of the room, a sure sign that she had found something. I took off trotting in the direction of her alert riffs and found her staring up at a weird-looking contraption on a shelf with six stout protruding handles. Belinda followed and stood beside me as we studied the thing.

"It looks like a body bag," Belinda announced.

"It is!" I had discovered a tastefully written sign and read the name of the company: Funeral Inspirations.

"Leslie." Belinda had that weary warning tone to her voice.

"Hey, this is interesting." I continued to read the sign which was all done up with lovely printing-type fonts and artwork. "'A body bag can be a low-cost option for burial or cremation, and comes in a variety of colors'—a very entrepreneurial idea, Belinda. Not only that, but these people even offer Contemporary Eco Coffins. If you fancy something very different, there are a couple of contemporary, very environmentally friendly options that mix style, design, and traditional techniques. There's a company called Sunset Coffins—figures it would be in the UK. They're much further along on this green stuff than we are over here." I continued reading, "'The unique green choice for those who care about the environment. Made in the UK from one hundred percent recycled newspaper board. Eight different colors to choose from.' They even used that British way of spelling *colors*. How classy is that? I guess the coffin disintegrates along with the body. You know, like when you buy a tomato plant and put the little environmentally friendly cardboard-type container in the hole along with the tomato. I am very impressed. People should know things like that are out there."

I glanced toward my best friend in the entire world. She was looking pretty green herself. I patted her on the arm. "That's okay; I keep forgetting how sensitive you are about funeral stuff."

As we made our way toward the exit, I stopped at a gigantic mahogany casket. "Hey, come look at this mahogany number. I'll bet this one costs a pretty penny. It looks like the one Marjorie rode home. This one has a hydraulic table. Too bad they didn't have Marjorie on one of these babies. It couldn't have been much of a picnic cranking her bulk up by hand." My finger hovered over the on switch.

"Leslie, don't you dare push that button. Let's go." She ground out the words between clenched teeth.

"I wasn't going to push the button, Belinda. Sheesh. What, you think I'm stupid? We're in here now; let's take advantage of the opportunity and really look around."

"We have already looked around, Les. You even managed to find disposable coffins, for heaven's sake. You should be a tour guide in here. Maybe you can apply for a job with that flirty funeral home director. The two of you could have a merry old time in here." Then she added in a strangled yelp, "Oh God, I get it now. I know how your mind works. Are you suggesting that man has that poor young woman, Katrina, crammed in one of these things?"

"Well, she wouldn't be 'crammed' in there...not if she's in there all by herself."

"Leslie Barrett, you are a ghoul. I'm going back to the car."

I was tapping my finger on the lid of the mahogany casket. "No, that isn't it. How many pounds do you think one of these things would hold?"

"Why?"

"Well, like I said...this one here looks like Marjorie's casket. Marjorie had to weigh about, what, close to three hundred pounds or so. One of those UK disintegrating coffins would never have accommodated Marjorie."

"Will you please stop making fun of Marjorie's obese remains? It is disrespectful."

"I'm not making fun of Marjorie. I'm working on a theory here." I drummed my acrylic nails on the coffin lid. "Now, Marjorie was a big girl. I'll bet they had to have a lot of pallbearers to get her to the grave site."

"Leslie..."

"Just hear me out; as much as that casket had to weigh with Marjorie inside, I would bet nobody would notice if it had gotten a little bit heavier between the time of the viewing and the burial." I looked at Belinda expectantly.

Her eyes rounded when she finally got my gist. "No...no...no..." Her voice was a harsh whisper. "You cannot be suggesting that man killed Katrina and rolled her in on top of Marjorie?! Oh, for heaven's sake, Leslie. Not only is that horrible, it is ridiculous!"

"Not on top of her." I made tucking motions with my hands. "But maybe, you know, to use your own words, crammed, shmooshed down in there somehow next to Marjorie. Katrina was a very thin girl. It would take a lot of cramming and shmooshing, but I believe it would be doable."

"You're certifiable. I swear, it's too bad this country has moved away from warehousing crazy people. I would love to be able to drive up to the entrance of the state hospital and set you on the doorstep. 'Here, would you please take my crazy best friend? I can't deal with her any longer.'"

"Very nice, Belinda. I'm not crazy; I'm just thorough." The tone of my voice was as dry and stiff as the room's vehicles. The *tick-tick-tick* of Riff's toenails could be heard coming from the depths of the room, only adding to the overall spookiness of the place.

"There must be thirty or forty coffins in here. We'll be here all night if we try to check every one of them. I'll bet it takes some muscle to raise the lids on these things. They really ought to have remote controls or something."

"Stop it. Just stop it. Katrina is not…" She stopped abruptly, and we gave each other identical looks of alarm at the crunch of hard-soled boots on gravel. "Somebody's coming," she hissed. "Find Riff; we've got to hide."

"What…where? I'm not climbing into one of these things. Riff… Riff…" I whispered for my dog.

Riff stuck her nose out from behind the wheels of the hydraulic gurney thing that was holding up the mahogany coffin. I one-handed her. "I've got Riff."

Belinda jogged around the large coffin. "Here, Leslie, get up on this table and lie down as flat as you can. He won't be able to see us over the coffin. "

Hugging Riff, I followed Belinda to an empty gurney that stood behind the mahogany coffin. She was right…that coffin would surely block his view. As long as he didn't wander around, we should be all right. Following orders, I tried to scramble onto the table with Riff in my arms. I let out a little "Eek" when Belinda planted her hand against my rear end and gave me a boost. She rolled onto the table behind me. Belinda is a very capable woman.

I whimpered, "The lights."

"Don't worry about them. Just be quiet."

We huddled together, practically spooning on the table. Although the room was well air-conditioned, I felt a trickle of sweat slide down my neck. The metal table felt cool against the side of my face. I prayed that Riff wouldn't start to whine. As a whimper escaped me, Belinda reached over my shoulder and clapped a hand over my mouth, which I did not appreciate but understood it as necessary.

I have never been so frightened in my entire life. I was shaking so badly that I imagined the table would start singing from the vibration. Belinda craned her neck to peer around the end of the casket. Belinda's courage never ceases to amaze me, so I drummed up some of my own and peaked under her chin. It was him, the groundskeeper guy. We watched as he entered the structure casually with a shovel in his hand, crossed to a large cabinet/closet/storage thing, opened a door, and shoved the shovel inside. He then snapped the door closed, strode toward the exit, and swiped an indifferent hand across the light switch. The room was plunged into an inky blackness, and the door closed with a loud bang.

A dead bolt slid home. "He's locking the door," I sniveled, and Belinda shushed me.

The heavy footsteps receded, and I was unable to maintain my shushed status. "Belinda, we are locked in here. Oh. My. God. It's dark as a cave in here. We are going to die…alone…in the dark. I think I'm going to hyperventilate."

"We aren't alone. We're in here together. Just be quiet and wait," she commanded softly.

I waited. Eventually, there was the sound of a vehicle's engine and the retreating sound of tires on gravel.

Heaving a relieved sigh, Belinda scrambled off the table.

"Here, Belinda, take Riff," I whispered, and dangled Riff in front of me in the darkness. Riff's slight weight left my hand and I was scooting my butt to the edge of the table when, like magic, Belinda produced a faint glowing light.

"Oh," I breathed, "you're a genius."

I immediately fished my cell phone from my pocket and flipped it open to reveal its puny light. Sometimes really stupid things fall out of my mouth. "You know, in the movies people walk into a pitch-black room, light one candle, and violà, the whole room is lit up. I always think, '*Boy, that must be one strong candlewick.*'"

"Good grief, Leslie, will you please shut up. Let's go," Belinda commanded, and I padded softly behind the bobbing dim cell phone light of my best friend, my dog cradled in her arm.

When we reached the door, it was just a huge gray blur. We didn't dare turn on the big lights again for fear of discovery, and I couldn't see crap with my puny cell phone lantern.

Where's a candle with a s trong wick when you need one?

Belinda handed Riff to me and fumbled with the door until I heard the solid *thunk* of a dead bolt. "Yay!" I cheered softly.

Belinda shoved open one of the double-hung doors, stuck her head out, and turned her head left, then right. "Come on, Les."

Riff and I sidled out the door behind her. We'd been inside that horror chamber for at least half an hour, and it was beginning to get pretty dark outside.

We made our way back to the Riviera. Hauling open the passenger door, I lightly tossed Riff inside and climbed in after her. Belinda and I sank into our respective seats and buckled up. Starting the car, Belinda heaved a sigh of relief. "Let's go home."

"We aren't going anywhere. That was the most fun I've had since Abner fell out of the scooper machine."

I convinced Belinda to cruise around the cemetery grounds for a bit, hoping to find Katrina's little Rio parked behind a huge gravestone or something. Those Rio cars are cute, but they sure are small. Riff and I got out at a couple of mausoleum-type structures and jogged around them, but we didn't find the Rio.

"What do you think he did with her car?" Belinda asked when Riff climbed back inside after we struck out at yet another mausoleum.

"He probably drove it to the airport and left it in the long-term parking lot. It could sit there for weeks before anyone would notice it." I widened my eyes at my friend, hoping she would catch my drift.

"Don't say it. I know what you're thinking. Don't say it."

I said it. "Surely that TBI agent thought to check the long-term parking at the airport in Knoxville. The Rio has a little bitty trunk, but…"

"I asked you not to say it. You need to watch reruns of Andy Griffith or something instead of all those creepy forensic shows."

I shrugged. "I can't help it. I like mysteries."

"Those shows are creepy…except for *NCIS*. Mark Harmon is cute."

"At the heart of all those shows, Belinda, is a mystery. And, yes, Mark Harmon is cute."

Once we left the cemetery grounds, we circled the block and parked next to the curb on Rivers Street, a few yards from one of the street-lights. Belinda cut the motor and turned off the headlights. We were once again sporting our night vision glasses.

"Ooooooooo," we agreed as the night swallowed our vehicle.

The jacket was getting hot, so I took it off and tossed it into the backseat where a delighted Riff pawed it into a doggie bed and settled down with a contented sigh.

We sat quietly as the night deepened around us. Both of us kept taking off our glasses, looking around, and putting them back on. The almost ghostly amber-tinted vision brought objects into sharp focus. Well, around light sources anyway. In the pure dark, everything looked pretty, purely dark. The graveyard itself was a sea of black broken by the hulking gray of headstones protruding from the earth like boulders from middle earth. There were some streetlights interspersed along the length of the drive, but they were so far apart they were practically useless. Little pockets of pooled light along the drive, and some vaporous lights next to the funeral home, were the only sources of light other than the moon. There was some transient bleeding of light onto the casket store from the security lights. I tried looking through the binoculars, but it was awkward due to the night vision glasses, and without them I couldn't see anything at all except a close-up of the vaporous lights.

"Here, Belinda"—I offered her the binoculars—"look at the lights near the funeral home through these without your night vision glasses, then try it with them on."

"No."

"Well, fine," I huffed. Replacing my glasses, I peered through the binoculars. "That's better."

"Seriously?"

"Yes, seriously."

"Let me see."

"No."

I relented, and we entertained ourselves for a while by staring into the darkness of the cemetery with and without the glasses. We were bored fairly quickly.

There is something about sitting in the dark with your best friend that encourages personal disclosure. "I think Quinn Braddock is very handsome too."

Belinda took off her glasses and gave me a contemplative look. "What is with you and Quinn Braddock all of a sudden?"

I shrugged. "Nothing, I just find him to be an attractive man. Do you ever think you could be interested in another relationship?"

"Oh God, no. Frank was enough for me. I cannot imagine putting that much energy into another man."

I laughed. "Yeah, I know what you mean. I still like to look though, and Quinn is mighty nice to look at."

"Sure. I enjoy perusing the salad bar, but I don't have to have a salad."

"Tom and I were married for almost forty years. If I married another man for forty years, that would mean I would have to live to be 108 years old. I can't live to be 108 years old. Social Security is supposed to go belly up by 2030."

"You're so silly." My friend laughed.

"That was nice, putting the twenty-third Psalm on Marjorie's tombstone. What did you put on Frank's tombstone?"

"Under his full name and dates of birth and death, I had them inscribe 'We will always remember.'"

"Ain't that the truth?"

"Leslie, be nice. Frank was a good man and a good prosecutor. You never did like Frank."

"Nope."

"I liked Tom."

"So did I."

"What are you going to do with Tom's ashes? You can't just leave the man in your closet for eternity."

"Why not? Tom isn't hurting anyone by being in my closet."

"What do you have engraved on his shoe box: 'Size 5½ Wide'?"

"Tom is not in a shoe box. Tom is in a very dignified box of his own that is next to a shoe box. When I figure out what I want to do with him, I'll tell you. Maybe I'll hijack a golf cart on a rainy day, get drunk, and go whooping around the country club, flinging Tom's ashes all over the fairway."

"That sounds like fun. Count me in. I will be the designated driver."

"It's a date."

We smiled at each another. Widowhood is no fun. But it's less lonely with another widow.

Chapter Twelve

We'd been quiet for a while when I asked Belinda, "So, you were an ER nurse. Did you ever find any dead bodies? I found a dead body one time."

"I know about your one-and-only dead body, Les. You've told me that story about a million times."

"I thought I'd found another one when Mr. Fischer didn't answer my *yoo-hoo*."

"I know; you told me about Mr. Fischer."

"I crept through the house and into the bedroom. There he was, just like Mrs. Weatherford, lying in the bed. Only Mr. Fischer was turned on his side."

"I know."

"I shook his shoulder gently, and that old randy coot rolled over. 'Well, hello there.' He grinned up at me." I shook my head and giggled, remembering. "Randy old coot."

"You just enjoy telling your dead-body stories, don't you?"

"At least I've found one. You didn't answer me. Did you find any dead bodies?"

"No, but I saw a lot of little kids with their heads stuck in one thing or another."

"No kidding? Janie got her head stuck in our stair rail when she was two. Tom, being an engineer and all, figured out the mechanics and slipped her right out. Carrie and I were hysterical, of course."

"I saw children with their heads stuck in aluminum pots, mixing bowls, wastebaskets, purses. You name it, and some kid got their head stuck in it."

"How did you get them out?"

"What happens is, the child gets upset and starts crying, which causes the head to swell, so most of the time a mild sedative allows the child to relax enough to slip them from whatever contraption they had been investigating at the time of their entrapment. We normally administered a mild sedative to the parents as well." She added, smiling at the memory, "It all depended on what the vessel was, of course. Sometimes we could cut the thing off the child's head. But that's tricky when you've got a small child screaming and wiggling around."

"Some little kid who lived across the street from us got a soup pot stuck on her head. My mom greased her up good with Crisco, and it slipped right off. I don't know why, but everybody in the neighborhood came to get my mom in a crisis."

"You told me that your mother was a nurse in World War Two, didn't you?"

"Yes."

"Well, there you go. Nurses are go-to people."

"But you never discovered a dead body?"

"No, Leslie, I'm sorry to have to admit that I never came upon a deceased patient. Some of the patients entering the ER were already dead, and some expired before the doctors could do anything for them; but I didn't do the kind of nursing where one makes rounds and then goes, 'Oh shoot, here's another dead body; now I've got a whole bunch of paperwork to do.' Believe it or not, Leslie, a lot of people go through their entire lives without being the first on the scene at the demise of a fellow human being. So, you can consider yourself lucky, or special, or cursed, or whatever."

I took off my glasses, looked around again, then put them back on.

"I haven't seen a thing. Have you?"

She mimicked my routine with the glasses and admitted she hadn't seen anything either.

"This is getting boring." I sighed. "I should have brought some coffee and doughnuts. On TV the cops always have coffee and doughnuts on a stakeout."

"No, coffee would only make you need to pee."

"Well, maybe just doughnuts then." I blew out a bored breath. "My dad used to say that cemeteries were very popular, in fact…"

"People are just dying to get in there." We finished the old joke together. Our laughter ended abruptly when lights from an approaching vehicle lit us up from behind and washed over the Riviera.

"Belinda, get down."

I almost slid under the dashboard, and Belinda scrunched her tall self as much as was humanly possible. "It's a truck, Les."

The truck turned into the entrance to the cemetery and immediately cut its lights. "Oh, that's suspicious, turning off the lights like that. Do you suppose it's that guy's truck?"

"It's difficult to tell. That's some serious dark out there. Even the night vision glasses don't cut through that kind of dark."

We watched with interest as the vehicle coasted slowly down the drive, momentarily spotlighted as it passed beneath the intermittent street-lights. It looked like a ghost truck creeping along. When it reached the funeral home, it stopped under one of the security lights.

Someone climbed from the truck cab, and I started focusing the binoculars. "Darn it, all I see is a lumpy shape. Whoever it is looks tall. This could be our guy."

The security light blinked off, and another one farther away came on. "Oh, that's just great. They must be on timers."

"Can you see him at all, Les?"

"Not really, just shapes and movement. It looks like he's dragging something." I heard a sound. "Did you hear that, Belinda? Turn the key to activate the windows. Lower my window."

Riff chose that moment to rejoin the party and leaped into my lap, placing her front paws on the door. "Riff hears it too."

"I don't hear anything except crickets," Belinda admitted in a hushed voice.

Then we all heard it: a squeaking and thumping from the location of the truck, followed by some short bursts of light, as though from a powerful flashlight.

"Belinda, those sound like muffled screams. It looks like he's moving deeper into the cemetery."

"Don't be ridiculous. I don't hear anything except for some squeaking and thumping."

"Seriously, Belinda, those could be the muffled cries of a young woman in distress. That looks like a pretty powerful flashlight he's using too." I reached over and powered up the window. I held Riff aloft with my left hand. "Here, you hold Riff; I'm going to see if I can get closer."

"Oh no you don't, Leslie Barrett. You are not getting out of this vehicle."

"I can't just sit here while a girl's life could be in danger."

"You promised that you wouldn't get out of the vehicle."

"I lied." I started yanking on the door handle with my right hand while still holding Riff aloft with my left. "Here, take Riff."

Belinda twisted and fished out her heavy flashlight. Accepting Riff with one hand, she thrust the flashlight at me with the other. "Here… if you must go, take my big flashlight."

"That thing is too heavy. I'll take the plastic one so it doesn't slow me down and leave the binoculars. They're no good to us now." I started struggling with the door again.

"Leslie, we should call 911 and let the police take over."

"We don't have anything to tell them other than a dark truck entered the cemetery and cut its lights, we heard squealing and thumping sounds, and we observed what appears to be somebody skulking through the graveyard with a powerful flashlight. The police will just assume it's some kids messing around."

"How will I know when it *is* time to call 911?"

"I'll turn the flashlight on and off twice when I want you to call 911. You return two flashes with your flashlight to confirm that you received the message."

"Leslie, we can't go flashing lights all over the place. You might as well jump up and down hollering, 'Over here, Mr. Possible Kidnapper/Killer, we're over here!'"

"I see your point."

"Just take your cell phone."

"Oh yeah, I left it in the pocket of Tom's coat." I twisted and half launched my body into the backseat to recover the phone. Jamming it into the pocket of my jeans, I promised, "I'll call you if I need help."

"Be careful. Don't draw attention to yourself."

"I'll be careful, Belinda. Wish me luck." I grasped the door handle, threw my shoulder into the heavy door—and the car interior lit up the night.

There wasn't much I could do except go with the momentum. The heavy door pulled me from the vehicle. I did my best to dance around the door, planted my feet in the dirt on the shoulder of the road, and shoved the door as hard as I could with both hands. I was rewarded with a very loud *THUNK!*

Very slick maneuvering, Leslie.

I froze with arms splayed and my back against the car door for an eternity, waiting for something to happen. Nothing happened. Thanks to the high-definition night vision glasses, I could see the darkness quite clearly. It was very clearly dark.

I risked a short blast from the flashlight to get my bearings. Once again in darkness, I darted through the ditch alongside the road and moved stealthily toward the tombstones. Once on the landscaped grounds I took high, long steps to avoid tripping on anything, such as those low-to-the-ground grave markers.

I worked up a rhythm of brief light bursts followed by long goose steps. In this fashion I wound my way—respectfully—around granite markers until I was maybe fifty feet from the street. Stopping in front of a tombstone as large as a one-car garage door, I ran the flashlight across the face of the stone. HAROLD GIVENS was prominently engraved. Harry had been dead for thirty-five years.

"Excuse me, Harry," I whispered foolishly. Harry had a gigantic, black marble rock. It was impressive. A daredevil could probably rappel up and down that rock. I toggled off the light and made my way around the stone, scraping my hand on the sharp granite. With a low curse I shook off the sharp pain.

I stood with my back against Harry's rock for a few seconds trying to figure out my next move. I had managed to get close enough so that the ambient wash from the security lights around the funeral home gave more definition to the suspect. The shadowy figure was indeed dragging something, and that something was making the squeaking and thumping noises.

What, or who, is he dragging?

I fished out my phone and punched up Belinda's pre-programmed cell phone number, wincing as I heard the trill of her phone in the car. Fortunately it only lasted about half a second before she pounced on it.

In a hushed, furtive voice, Belinda answered, "Leslie, are you all right. Come back to the car while you have the chance."

"No. I'm already out here now. He's dragging something into the cemetery." I matched my friend's hushed tone.

"Oh my God!" Belinda squealed.

"Shhhhh. I'm going to make my way toward the casket store. Maybe I can see more with the aid of the security lights."

"You can't do that; Leslie, he'll see you. Come back to the car."

"Hush. We can't risk the Riviera's inside light again. Just stay dark."

"Oh God. I don't like this. I'm calling 911."

"Not yet. I can't tell what it is I'm seeing here."

"Okay," she whispered reluctantly, "but keep this line open."

"Good thinking." I had a firm grip on the cell phone, being careful to shield the lit side against my body. I waited a few beats, then made a run for it. Catching the toe of my Keds on one of the low-to-the-ground granite markers, I pitched headlong into the night.

As my cell phone sailed from my hand like a spiraling lightning bug, my chin smacked the ground, and I rolled with the pain. Somehow I managed to hold on to the flashlight. I lay stunned for a couple of seconds, then quickly scrambled around until I spotted the faint glow of my phone, belly crawling toward it. Before I even reached the thing, I could hear Belinda through the tiny speaker freaking out in the car. "LESLIE. LESLIE. WHAT HAPPENED? LESLIE... OH GOD!"

Snatching the phone from the grass, I whispered fiercely, "Calm down. I'm all right; I just tripped on a flat tombstone."

"Leslie, come back to the car this instant. You're giving me a heart attack here," she wheezed.

"I'm going to take a look around the casket store first. I think he's too preoccupied with what he's doing to have heard anything. He's still moving deeper into the cemetery."

"There is nothing in that casket building except for caskets, Leslie. Come. Back. To. The. Car," she hissed.

"Not yet," I hissed back. I started to stand but dropped again to the ground with my joints howling bloody murder when I realized the man was heading back to the funeral home. He was still dragging something, but now the something was large and wobbly, causing him to stop every few steps to resettle the something. I shuddered at the thought that Katrina had been stashed somewhere on the cemetery grounds, in a mausoleum perhaps? Once the large whatever tumbled to the ground, and I watched him return it to some kind of wheeled platform. This was not looking good for Katrina. I stayed on my belly so the white part of the Corvette on my t-shirt wouldn't give me away.

Suddenly I heard something big padding toward me from behind, making snuffling noises.

Oh sweet mother of God! All I could think was *BEAR!* I rolled into a ball and tried to cover my head with my arms, conking myself with the plastic flashlight in the process. The snuffling got louder and came closer. I was quaking with fear and, unable to quell my terror, squeaked into the phone, "Bear...bear...bear..." when a cold nose probed my ear and a wet sandpaper tongue licked me right on the face...which I hate. I peeked through my hands. It was a dog, a big-guy dog, and he was evidently delighted to see me.

"Go away," I whispered urgently. "Shoo, go away."

"A BEAR? OH MY GOD, DID YOU SAY A BEAR? ROLL UP IN A BALL, ROLL UP IN A BALL AND PROTECT YOUR HEAD!" She was shouting into the phone.

"It's okay. I'm okay. Hush. It's just some big, stupid dog wandering around out here. He scared me," I whispered into the phone, feeling like an absolute moron.

"Leslie. Come. Back. To. The. Car. NOW!"

"No, Belinda, he's headed toward the funeral home, hauling something or someone behind him. Hold on. Stay quiet, and stay dark."

Belinda gave a horrified squeak. "Shhhhhh…" I cautioned, but could still hear her ragged breathing.

"Go away," I whispered to the dog. "Shoo…nice doggy, go home, shoo." Finally losing interest in the crazy woman, the dog wandered off among the hulking tombstones.

The man stopped at the back of the truck and left the squeaking/thumping something unattended. He walked behind the funeral home to where the casket store waited. The second I lost sight of him, I leaped to my feet and sprinted across the manicured lawn with my flashlight beam leading the way.

From the open phone in my left hand, I heard my friend's frantic cries, "Leslie, is that you running with the light? Are you okay? Come back to the car!"

I ignored my friend's anguished cries and vaulted the curb. I scampered across the driveway, half-wanting to go to the aid of the something waiting behind the truck and half-terrified for my own safety. I scooted to the security of the funeral home and snugged my back against its front. I decided to circle the funeral home and come at him from the opposite side.

Halfway across the front of the building, I stopped to catch my breath and whispered desperately to my friend, "Belinda, I'm hanging up now. Call 911. I'm going around the funeral home to keep an eye on him." All I heard before I punched the off button was Belinda's now-familiar gerbil-like squeal.

When I reached the far side of the funeral home, I hustled to the rear of the building and slithered around the corner with my flashlight now turned off. I crunched over the gravel as quietly as possible, constantly swiveling my head in search of the man, but he was nowhere to be seen. Having safely traversed the gravel drive without incident, I crept down the side of the casket store toward the rear of the building. As I drew closer I heard rustling and clanking sounds. My finger poised over the flashlight's on button, I peeked around the corner, then mashed the button. A woman swung toward me in the flare of light with a startled gasp.

I whispered raggedly, my voice as gravelly as the driveway, "Katrina... Katrina? Is that you?"

A man's voice called out, "Who's there?"

What are you doing, Leslie? Get out of here. In full agreement with myself, I raced toward the front of the building, rounded the corner, and ran smack into the big creep.

Strong hands gripped my forearms, and a furious, growling voice demanded, "What's going on here. Who are you?" In one swift movement, my night vision glasses and wool cap were swept from my head.

My scream would have made Jamie Lee Curtis proud. In the pool of light from the security lights, there was no doubt that this was the man who had been stalking Katrina...the man who had approached Belinda and me outside the casket store...the jerk with the nice wife and cute kid living in a house on Rivers Street.

I gave a mighty kick to his shin, but apparently a size 5½ Keds'-shod foot doesn't incapacitate a grown man, because all he did was say "Ow."

I thrashed furiously in his grasp, cursing and shouting, "What have you done with Katrina? Where is she, you, you,...YOU?"

He yelled, "Lady, I don't know what you're yelling about! What's going on?"

I twisted my right hand and raked my tenpenny fingernails across his forearm. He released me quickly with a little push and a yelp of pain.

I hopped onto the gravel lane that runs between the buildings and scrambled away from his solid, hulking form. As I took off running, he hollered, "HEY! YOU OVER THERE! WHO ARE YOU? STOP, THIEF!"

I went screaming in a zigzag sprint down the lane, slipping and sliding on the gravel, fully expecting to feel the slam of a bullet against my spine. Belinda's black Riviera tore around the corner of the funeral home, spewing gravel, headlights blazing, and aimed right for me.

"BELINDA...HELP!" I bawled in unashamed terror.

Belinda screeched to a stop, and I continued on past the Riviera and around to the back of the vehicle. That stupid dog who had nuzzled me earlier came loping over and slapped two big paws on my chest, shoving my back against the trunk. The big, dumb dog was panting happily in my face.

My best friend in the entire world flung open the driver's door, planted her feet on the blacktop, pointed the heavy flashlight directly at the perpetrator, and shrieked at the top of her lungs, "FREEZE, MOTHER FRICKER!"

Riff leaped from the Riviera and ran fearlessly toward the killer, whose back was now turned toward me—and right past him toward a shadowy figure lurking near the far corner of the casket store. Riff started barking bullets, *arf!arf!arf!arf!arf!arf!arf,* lifting herself from the gravel drive with each fierce *arf.* The stupid graveyard dog just continued to smile and slurped me on the face—which I hate.

The blare of police sirens was deafening. My head swiveled as a cruiser rounded one side of the funeral home and another cruiser came from the other side so they were facing each other, with Belinda, the Riviera, the man, Riff, the shadowy figure, the graveyard dog, and me sandwiched in between.

I stared at my hand stupidly and wondered why it was bleeding. Leaning back against the trunk and into the dog, I sank slowly to my butt. For the first time since being bonked on the head playing dodgeball at the age of seven, I passed out.

Chapter Thirteen

Riff was still barking, and a stern male voice demanded, "Somebody shut that dog up!" The harsh command implied Riff-Raff was being less than helpful and brought me part of the way back. I blinked up at Belinda, who was dabbing cotton against my chin.

Scrambling in place, I grabbed her hand with both of mine. "Belinda...Belinda...my God, are you okay? Is Katrina okay?"

"I'm okay, Les," Belinda said warmly. "We didn't find Katrina, but we did catch a thief." She proceeded to dab again at my chin.

"Ow"—I swept her hand away from my face—"that hurts."

"Show me your hand, Leslie," she ordered, and I complied. She started scrubbing at me again with a new cotton pad.

"Ow-ow-ow." I shook my hand at the stinging antiseptic. Belinda must have gotten her nurse bag from the trunk. Always prepared, that's my friend.

Riff started barking again, and I cased the crowd. She was dancing around the feet of a middle-age woman who was being handcuffed by a City of Clifton policeman. Another officer yelled, "Would somebody *PLEASE* come get this dog!"

"Stop yelling at my dog!" I hollered, struggling to get to my feet. Belinda stepped back, and the officer helped me stand up. "Here, Riff!"

She immediately stopped barking bullets in the woman's direction and raced into my arms. I buried my face in her fur and crooned, "Oh, Riff, you were so brave, baby. Are you okay?" She started licking my face, which I hate. "Okay, okay, that's enough." I moved her out of face-licking range.

"Why are they arresting that lady, Belinda? Who is she?" I had no idea what was going on.

Suddenly I recognized Quinn Braddock in the crowd of cops. "What's Quinn doing here?"

He was talking with the groundskeeper, who stood with one hand in the front pocket of his blue jeans and one hand on the head of the graveyard dog.

I hollered at the man, "Where's Katrina?"

"He doesn't have Katrina, Les." Belinda put her arm around my shoulder. "We made a mistake about that man and Katrina."

"We did?"

I hollered at the groundskeeper, "I'm sorry. I thought you were a killer! My mistake! Nice dog."

The dog was a black Lab…no wonder he was so friendly. There is a reason Labrador retrievers aren't trained as police dogs. A cop commands, "Go get him," and the Lab comes romping back with an old baseball it found discarded in the grass.

Belinda pointed at a cruiser backing down the gravel lane. "The police arrested that woman. After a funeral and burial, she would come and load up her truck with the flowers and plants and stuff. She was robbing Marjorie Vickers tonight."

"That's terrible." I huffed, staring indignantly at the departing vehicle.

"Then she was turning around and selling the stolen stuff at the Saturday flea market here in Clifton." Belinda grinned down at me. "She had a sweet little racket going, and we put a stop to it."

Comprehension dawned. "The lights in the cemetery, the ones residents were reporting, that Quinn was telling us about, that was her, right?"

"Right, Les. We caught her. The police are quite pleased with us."

I grinned back at Belinda. "Well then, our efforts have not been in vain." I noticed she had her night vision glasses perched on her head and frowned. "Hey, where are my glasses?"

Both of us looked around, and I saw two officers playing around with them. They were trading them back and forth and looking at stuff. "Hey, you guys! Quit playing with my glasses. You'll get them all stretched out of shape. I might need those again!" In a side voice I said, "Belinda, make them give me back my glasses, please."

"I will, Les. If they stretch them out, we'll get you another pair. They are too valuable a tool to be without."

"You are so right, Belinda. It must be because of the advanced HD lens technology; wouldn't you agree?"

"Absolutely."

Quinn walked toward us, talking on a cell phone. "Leslie, Agent Donnelly wants to talk to you."

"Who?"

"Hailey Donnelly, you know, the lady agent with the TBI."

"Oh, Hailey. I forgot about Hailey." To Belinda I added, "Sorry, Belinda, I forgot to tell you that I called and left her a message before we started out tonight, just in case we needed some backup."

I reached for the cell phone. "Hello, Hailey, yes, yes, Belinda and I are fine. Unfortunately, we didn't find Katrina, but we have managed to stop a crime spree here in Clifton."

In my ear, Hailey sputtered, "Mrs. Barrett, are you totally out of your mind?"

Boy, talk about sour grapes. Just because we wrap-ped this up before she got here.

"No, I don't believe so," I replied staunchly.

Hailey announced dramatically, "Katrina Stephens returned to her dorm room this afternoon. She had been with some guy in Oak Ridge. She is fine."

"Oh good, that *is* a relief." I shared the good news with Belinda. "Katrina has turned up safe and sound."

"Thank goodness!"

Into the phone I said, "Look, Hailey, thank you for calling, but everything is under control. I don't have time to talk with you just now. Here's Quinn; he can fill you in." I handed the cell phone back to Braddock.

"What was that all about?" Belinda plucked Riff from my arms.

"I don't know." I sniffed, "She's got her panties in a bunch over something. Can we go home now?"

Chapter Fourteen

I was a little banged up at the end of the evening, with a scraped chin, a scraped hand, and a sore spot on my head where I'd clocked myself with the plastic flashlight. The man I had mistaken for kidnapping and/or killing Katrina Stephens turned out to be Paul Duncan, a member of the maintenance crew at Walton's cemetery. When I collided with him at the entrance of the casket store, he'd been on a little snooping expedition of his own. Paul had worked at Walton's for ten years and was furious about the (literal) grave robbing, and even more frustrated by the lack of progress by the authorities. Living directly across the street from the cemetery with his lovely wife, charming little girl, Rufus the graveyard dog, and raucous wind chimes, he had been keeping an eye out for suspicious activity in the cemetery. Alerted by the night's light show—that is, the Riviera lighting up like a road flare, and me running and tumbling all over the place—he set out with his black Lab to investigate.

Paul had been loitering outside Marjorie's viewing room because the funeral home director had requested Paul make himself available to assist the pallbearers in moving Marjorie to the grave site. He had no interest whatsoever in Katrina. Katrina later admitted that she never stopped at the cemetery after she left Marjorie's house but had driven directly to her *friend's* apartment in Oak Ridge. Belinda and I were just relieved that the young woman had never been in danger.

Quinn was there the night of our takedown because some of the officers from the Glen had volunteered to help the Clifton police with their frequent cruising of the cemetery grounds. Subsequent clarification with Quinn revealed that the conversation Belinda had overheard that day in the Public Safety office had been about the increasing volume of thefts at the cemetery, including large floral *sprays* and *vases* of flowers. The thief was fifty-five-year-old Agnes Knight. Agnes used a wagon to haul her stolen booty from the grave site to her small pickup truck. A large, lovely azalea bush kept toppling off the wagon as she trundled her way from Marjorie's final resting place. It was the azalea bush that I had mistaken for an incapacitated Katrina. I had also mistaken the squealing and thumping of her old, worn wagon for screams of help…again coming from an incapacitated and possibly muzzled Katrina disguised as an azalea bush.

When I ran into Quinn at the Dollar General, I asked whether he had heard from Agent Donnelly. He mumbled something and became suddenly enamored of a display of birthday cards. I found this to be a curious response to a legitimate question. I thought Agent Hailey Donnelly and I had formed a liaison of sorts, but perhaps I was mistaken.

Three weeks after our latest adventure, Belinda called to inform me that the Wildlife Resources Agency had captured our bear.

"Are they sure that it was our bear? How can they tell one black bear from another one?"

"Leslie, they cornered the bear on someone's deck over on Lanchester Drive. That's only two streets over from us. They're sure that it is the same bear who's been rummaging around our area."

"Well, that's a relief. I hope the bear didn't get too comfortable around here. I wouldn't want it to come back next year."

"It won't come back next year, Les."

"Belinda, I have done extensive research on bears, and they are very territorial. Once a bear has a defined food source, it tends to keep coming back, and the Glen is riddled with bird feeders."

"The wildlife people euthanized the bear, Leslie."

I inhaled in horror. "No! Why? That is terrible. From all the pictures people were snapping of him, he was such a scrawny little bear." I could feel my eyes welling up. I like animals—I don't like alligators or tarantulas, and I wouldn't like a grizzly bear hulking around the neighborhood—but the idea of eighty-sixing that puny little-guy bear was unacceptable.

"Leslie, don't get upset about it. I can hear it in your voice; you're getting upset about it. Listen, just the other day there was a lady in the news in Florida; she was attacked by a bear and almost dragged into the woods. The bear had her head in its mouth, for crying out loud!"

I railed, "Well, sure, in *Florida*. A person can't walk anywhere in that state without encountering some sort of man-eating beast. But this is Tennessee, for cryin' out loud! Why didn't they just relocate him? I read in the Glen newspaper that the wildlife people are planning a goose roundup. If they can round up those stupid Canadian geese and bus them to Vancouver, why couldn't they drive one little underfed bear up into the Smoky Mountains or somewhere?"

"Leslie, you said yourself that once a bear established this area as his territory that he might keep coming back. And where there is one bear there may be others on the way. The wildlife people had no choice."

"I have no doubt that little bear would have encountered bird feeders close to the Smoky Mountains. It would have to be one determined bear to hoof its way back to the Glen. Besides, they could have taken him far away, chucked him out in Pennsylvania, out in the Poconos or somewhere. I hate this; I really do. This is just miserable."

"Who was going to drive one bear to the Poconos? Would you have volunteered to drive it to Pennsylvania?"

"We'll never know now, will we?"

Hello Readers,

Thanks for allowing Leslie & Belinda to inhabit your brain for a bit. They run around in mine like a couple of confined hamsters.

I hope you enjoyed my first book in the series. A brief review on Amazon, BN.com, Goodreads, or other review site would be appreciated.

It seems that Leslie & Belinda have already caught the scent of another mystery in the Glen. I can't wait to release the hamsters.

~ Linda

Follow me on:
Facebook: Linda S. Browning
Twitter: @LindaSBrowning
Website: lindabrowning.net

63274745R00082

Made in the USA
Lexington, KY
03 May 2017